Wilder Creatures

NADIA STEVEN RYSING

Undertaker Books

WILDER CREATURES

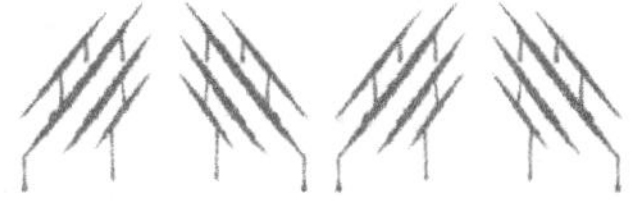

UNDERTAKER BOOKS
www.undertakerbooks.com

For everyone who aided a snow-struck traveler on Highway 6/Grey County Road 6 on December 25, 2022.

Thank you for helping us find our way home when we needed it most.

We all know, the end will come. You either face your hunters or run from them.

- David Adams Richards

CHAPTER ONE

A LL HER LIFE, RUTH had been slow to respond to a question. Whether it was her soft low voice, her overactive mind, or her deep-set knowledge that all answers may be wrong, Ruth met so much of the unexpected of her life with silence.

"Honey, did you hear what I said?"

Yes, Ruth had heard her mother, but her response was focused solely in her body. Her hand trembled as it held the receiver; she reflexively gritted her teeth in response. She leaned her head back on the exposed brick of her apartment wall. She breathed in practiced measurements—five seconds in, seven seconds out each time. She looked around the kitchen, counting each cupboard door until she was finally able to speak.

Ruth murmured, "Yeah, Mum, I heard you."

Her mother sighed. "Good. Now, I know it's sudden, but we're hoping to have the funeral tomorrow. There's supposed to be a cold snap next week so we need to...we need to be able to break the ground still. I know you're busy with school, so I understand if you can't get here in time, but—"

"I'll come home tonight," Ruth promised, leaning over to check the underutilized calendar on the wall opposite her. "I just have to make a few calls."

"It's just such a shock," her mother whispered. "My poor boy, my poor baby boy... You never expect these things, you never think that you'll live to bury your child. Ruth... Ruth, I can't see him like he is. You'll go for me, right? You'll tell them who he is?"

"I better go, Mum," Ruth murmured. "I'll text you when I get close."

Ruth hung up the phone without letting her mother say anything else. She put her face in her hands and breathed deeply.

You'll tell them who he is?

She had a long drive ahead of her. She couldn't think about that now.

It was an oddly quiet drive going back north. She normally would listen to the radio on such a long trip, but there was already too much going on in her head.

She didn't need more chatter.

She caught her reflection in the rearview mirror. Ruth could see the bags under her eyes, the lines on her brow from frowning too much recently. She wasn't even thirty—close, but not quite yet—but she looked like she had aged a few more decades since the last time she had been home.

She worried they would see that the minute she walked in the door. But that was better than them noticing her clear relief that her brother was dead.

Ruth stopped by the hospital first, reluctantly turning off the truck's engine. She paid for parking and went in through the front entrance. She saw the officers waiting for her and she nodded to them. They introduced themselves but she couldn't process it, her heart beat too loud to hear anything else as they stepped into the elevator together.

Ruth was led into the morgue, the coroner sitting at his desk. He stood, straightening the tie half tucked into his lab coat. If he tried to introduce himself, Ruth didn't notice. But the first officer spoke to him as the other attempted to soothe Ruth, warning her about what she was about to see. She flinched at his hand on her shoulder and he quickly pulled away. The coroner unlocked one of the panels of chrome lining the wall—he might have warned her too, but Ruth wasn't listening—and then revealed the chilled corpse waiting inside.

David lay on the gurney, his skin pale, his muscles stiff. They covered him the best they could, but she could see the hole in his chest. He was ripped apart, gutted. But there was no doubt in her mind: it was her brother. After a brief confirmation, she left. She had no interest in being there any longer.

When Ruth arrived at home, she found herself alone in the quiet, snow falling silently as she stepped out of the truck and into the driveway. She waited on the doorstep, looking up at the splintered wood. David wasn't there, but she could still hear his voice telling her to leave. She could still picture his eyes, the fire in them a steady ember of hate.

Ruth finally entered the silent house.

She should have expected this. Her mother lived down the road now on a small hobby farm. And with David gone, Ruth imagined her sisters would have moved over to Uncle Trip's place.

She found herself utterly exhausted and went upstairs, barely managing to throw off her coat as she went into her childhood room and lay down. Her hands went to her own ribs, her fingers tapping against the bones as her thoughts ran wild with the possibilities of what David looked like beneath that cloth. She could guess, based on how the fabric had draped over him, where it had dipped low into the deepest of his wounds.

Ruth had the old dream, the one she had almost every night the year she was sixteen. The buck across the whitened fields, the snow falling so thick she could barely see through it. David standing behind her, raising the rifle in her arms, as she closed one eye and aimed to fire. The moment would hold beyond the shot, just long enough for her to feel the recoil before forcing herself awake.

It was strange waking in that room, the walls now plastered with posters from a younger generation. David had been renovating the farmhouse for a few years now, but he hadn't changed anything upstairs yet. The bottom floor was slowly transforming, becoming more and more modern. A more nostalgic person would be in tears seeing the historical house changed into something out of a glossy magazine. But Ruth didn't care. A man's home was his home; he could do what he pleased with it.

Though, she thought quietly, it was hers now.

She didn't linger in bed. There was work to do, even in the winter. Chickens to feed, a cow to milk. There was a goat favoring his left hind leg, her mother had warned her. There would be enough things to do before the afternoon. Mum had insisted the visitation be there. Ruth would have to get ready.

The memorial was a quiet affair. They buried David on the property, not more than a strong stone's throw away from the house. There was a minister who sang her brother's praises. David's hard work, his faith, his commitment to family. He prayed over them all as her brother went into the soon-to-be-frozen ground. The minister walked among them, but he passed by Ruth without a second glance. His priority was for the openly grieving. Silent mourners were only of interest to gossips or to those who wanted to prove to themselves that they loved the deceased more than anyone else.

Ruth stood still as David's body was lowered, her teenage cousins struggling with the heavy coffin. Mum was curled into her frame, sobbing into her black jacket. Ruth's two sisters stood on the other side of the grave, both fingering the phones in their pockets like security blankets.

There was a hymn, but Ruth didn't know it.

The reception filled her house with black-clad strangers. Some she recognized. Neighbours, some from the church, some were even David's friends from school Ruth hadn't seen for years. She simply sat on the couch, letting them all pass by. Her younger sister Esther sat beside her, her head on Ruth's shoulder. Esther had grown so much since Ruth had last seen her, only a few months before. Her sister's tousled dirty blonde hair was hastily pulled back, her makeup as poorly done as only a fifteen-year-old girl can manage, barely covering up her remarkably freckled face.

Esther said quietly, "I don't want to be here."

Ruth put her arm around her younger sister and said, "We get to mourn when they leave. Can you keep it together until then?"

Esther nodded thoughtfully and Ruth kissed her on the forehead.

"Hang in there," Ruth murmured before rising from the couch.

"There you are," Mum called from the kitchen, obviously drunk as she walked out to her. "It's time for you to do a speech. Everyone else did one. Your turn, Ruth. Tell everyone about our David."

Ruth knew her mother wanted her to say something meaningful about her brother's life, how she loved him, how she missed him. But she had nothing she wished to share with polite society.

"I think you've had enough," Ruth replied quietly, taking her mother's glass of wine from her.

Ruth walked into the kitchen, blushing hard, as she poured the drink down the drain. She splashed some cold water on her face before turning back to face the room. She scratched her neck, the black wool dress irritating her skin.

Through the doorframe she saw Mum crying onto Esther's shoulder. Esther was perfectly attuned to their mother, curling in around her and rubbing her back.

Ruth left the kitchen, climbed up the stairs, and went into her old bedroom. She found Naomi lying on her stomach, her headphones in while she texted on her phone. At seventeen Naomi was growing to look more and more like Ruth, though still as freckled as Esther. She had recently dyed her hair black, though her red eyebrows still shone brightly against her skin.

"Out," Ruth ordered.

Naomi groaned as she sat up. "Rue, I just want to be alone. Please just let me stay up here."

"If I have to suffer through this bull so do you," Ruth retorted. "Downstairs, now."

Naomi finished the text and put her phone back in her pants pocket.

"I can't believe you even get reception out here," Ruth muttered.

"You'll need a different service provider," Naomi commented. "Unless you want to be stuck to a landline the entire time you're here."

Ruth frowned as they walked back down the stairs, seeing Mum now looking wistfully at a photo of Dad, her fingers stroking the glass.

Ruth heard the beginnings of a story, but left the room. She knew what her mother was going to say. She had heard it for years, every time Mum had the wrong amount of wine and the right amount of company. Ruth went to the door and put on her winter coat and boots as Mum gave her monologue.

"Your father was such a good man, girls, his heart was too big for his own chest, that's what they all said when it gave out. I wish he could have seen you grown; he was so proud, so proud of all of you. I miss him every day. But the Lord has His plan. He needed another angel, him and your brother both now. I don't understand why it wasn't me. A woman should not have to bury her husband and child."

Ruth didn't hear the rest before she passed through the door, left the main lawn, and headed into the grove. David was buried under a pine tree, an oddly pagan resting place considering her family's deep faith in non-denominational Christianity. It was quiet here, quieter than it had any right to be, and the new dusting of snow covered the trampling of the recent mourners. It was peaceful. It was the sort of peaceful someone might find solace in.

Ruth stood at the foot of his grave, her shoulders tight. She hadn't known what she would feel, standing above his body. She had feared unexpected grief or regret, but all that boiled in her was rage.

She hissed, "I know who you were. I don't care what she says. I don't care what any of them say. I know who you are, David, you bastard, and I'll never forget it. If they knew, they would have buried you another six feet. They should have kept digging until they reached hell and tossed you in. I hope you rot, David. I hope the animals drag you out and finish what they started. I hope I get to bury your mangled carcass again."

The wind whistled through the trees and the snow stirred around the small stone marking the spot. Her anger softened, her rage slipping into heartbreak. It was over. It was all over. That ire would only poison her further. This wasn't like her. She was smarter than this, smarter than her choice to run out of a wake to scream at a corpse.

So she took a deep breath and turned toward the house.

The silence broke as she heard her mother sobbing and the soft comforting of all those who feared death. She felt no compulsion to return to them. But still she went into the house and let others tell her how truly sorry they were for her loss.

CHAPTER TWO

THE NEXT MORNING, RUTH drank her coffee alone on the back porch steps, wrapped in her winter gear and a poorly knitted blanket as she looked across the property. A hundred acres. Not a large property, but enough to make a living. Her father had bought a second farm just before his death, ten kilometers down the lane. This was where Mum lived now. The girls had been living with David since they entered high school, their mother claiming that it was safer for them to get to school in the winter. Ruth knew that their mother preferred living alone, but she never told the girls this.

But David was dead now. Mum would not be able to look after them by herself. Naomi was nearly eighteen, but Esther was barely fifteen. They would need a place to live. Trip would only be able to watch them for so long. He and June had three boys of their own, all between the ages of twelve and sixteen. Two more teenagers might break them.

Ruth adjusted her hood as she looked out on the property. She could sell, certainly, but she knew she could not throw ancestral land away so easily. No one would let her. And now her brother was buried here. They would never abandon his body.

She adjusted her seat so the dog could pass her, running down the steps toward the nature reserve. Cora was just a little poodle, but she thought she could take on the entire wilderness herself. Ruth stood to chase after her, but remembered the fence between the two properties. While she was not particularly fond of dogs, she didn't have the heart to give Cora away. The girls would have enough trouble adjusting when they moved back in without losing their pet.

Ruth walked toward the chicken coops to investigate, drinking her coffee still. She entered, peering at the resting creatures, stepping over another hen before kneeling. Ruth heard a whistling and she took off her glove. She reached around until her fingers found a hole between the panels of the back wall. She pursed her lips, mentally noting to check the barn for cracks as well.

She heard a yelp and she left the coop, looking over the fields for the dog. She waited before calling out, "Cora!"

Only the winter wind answered her back.

Ruth went into the house, grabbing the rifle that hung above the kitchen door. She perched it on her shoulder as she walked out into the winter fields, her feet crunching in the snow as she followed the dog's footprints.

She made it to the edge of the property, seeing the mangled fence and an opening large enough for the dog to scoot under.

Ruth groaned and muttered, "Are you serious, David?"

She climbed over it the best she could, landing on her back in the snow. She saw the dog not far from her, whimpering as it ran past her, back toward the fence.

"What's gotten into you, mutt?" Ruth grumbled as something caught the corner of her eye. She froze, looking about for signs of a predator. It would be unusual for wolves or a cougar to be in the area, but creatures were known to do foolish things when they were hungry. David's body was proof enough of that.

When she heard nothing, she stepped forth, seeing a trail of prints. She knelt down, frowning as she made out the pattern. A human, not wearing any shoes, had come through the woods toward the farm and had turned back.

Ruth made her way back over the fence and held it up for Cora to slip under. She scooped the dog up and carried the trembling creature on her long walk back to the farmhouse.

Once they got back, Ruth went into the kitchen, putting the dog down on the floor and laying the gun on the kitchen table before pulling out her cell phone. She hit her newest contact and waited for the phone to connect, after an electronic voice reminded her it was a long-distance call.

"Constable Henley?" she asked. "It's Ruth MacGowan. I think there's something you ought to come and see."

Henley arrived a bit past 10 a.m. Ruth waited for him in the kitchen, brewing another pot of coffee as Cora whined by her feet. She threw the poodle a scrap of coffee cake, but the dog rejected the offering, instead lying down under the table and whimpering.

Ruth heard the knock and let the constable in, leading him through the back into the kitchen. He was a heavier man, with a bit of grey in his hair, and a generally pleasant disposition. The dog went to him, still whining, and he knelt to give her a pat.

"Good to see you again, little girl," he greeted. "I heard you had a bit of a scare today."

"Can I get you something to eat or drink?" Ruth offered. "We've got plenty left over from the funeral."

"That's kind of you," Henley replied, "but I'm fine. How are you handling all of this?"

"I'm alright," Ruth said curtly. "You said I should phone you if there was any more I could tell you about David."

"Of course," Henley said, "but I have to tell you, the investigation might be closing soon. There's no evidence of foul play. It seems like our initial instinct was right, it might have just been an animal attack. We've had reports of a momma black bear in the area. With the early winter, it wouldn't surprise me if David got too close and she went berserk."

Ruth grabbed the wire cutters and her coat. "I think there might be more to it than that. You'll want to put your gloves on for this."

She walked with Henley out toward the forests, the poodle in tow. When they got to the fence, Henley paused and said, "You could have just told me this. It looks like a bear could have done this. I don't see what—"

Ruth cut the wire fence the rest of the way and pulled it apart with her bare hands until it was big enough for Henley.

"Got to fix it anyway," she explained. "Come on."

She led him to the spot where she had found Cora and pointed toward the tracks. "Here, what do you see?"

"It's a footprint," he said, squinting. "It's a human. That's not—"

"It's barefoot," Ruth stated. "Do you see that? Probably a size six and my guess is either a small female or a real big kid."

Henley looked up at her. "What are you saying?"

"I think you're looking at a missing person's case," Ruth insisted. "My sister told you she heard someone that night, right? That she thought David was seeing someone and sneaking around."

"Yes—"

"And my brother was found not thirty feet from here, ripped apart." Henley looked down as Ruth insisted, "This wasn't a bear attack. This was someone getting even and making a point by doing it."

"Your brother was a respected man in this community," he replied, his voice breaking. "I don't know what you're suggesting, but if you're implying a footprint in the snow indicates your brother was in some...some...salacious business, then well, Miss—"

"What I'm saying here is that there is someone out here, someone was running away from here with no shoes. And I think you know my brother was no saint."

"You thought yourself it was a bear attack," Henley reminded her. "This fence only proves that further. Miss MacGowan... I know it's difficult losing a family member. I remember when my dad passed. ..you think there's something more to it, that there's got to be some meaning to it all. But sometimes, these things just happen."

Ruth felt a flush across her cheeks and she apologized. David was no paragon of virtue, but jumping to human trafficking was a stretch. "I'm sorry... I'm..."

Henley patted her on the shoulder awkwardly and said, "I'll bring a photo of this back to the station. I'll check and see if we have any missing persons in the area. Thank you for bringing this to my attention."

Ruth walked him back to the house and watched as the car drove off. She played it all through again. It didn't make any sense. That part of the property hadn't been fenced off before. It was a good few klicks before their property touched anyone else's and besides Cora none of the household would be stupid enough to go running around in the woods by themselves. It might make sense if David was trying to keep someone in, but...

Ruth shook her head, trying to get her thoughts together. Not a hostage situation. There were too many other people either living on or visiting the property. She doubted that David had gotten into something so seedy without someone noticing.

Ruth poured herself another cup of coffee and sat down at the kitchen table. She was being paranoid. She was bringing her own garbage into this when there was nothing. Whatever it had been, she had told the cops and that was that.

Ruth drank her coffee in silence, ignoring the tears starting to fall down her face. She should talk to someone. People talked to people about things like this. Trouble was, the people who knew David wouldn't get it and the people who would get it wouldn't give a shit about David. There was only one person she wanted to talk to and at that moment she was so shaken she was stupid enough to dial her number.

"Hello?" a sleepy voice asked.

"Hi Ellie," Ruth said, "it's me. Sorry, I forgot you would have been working last night. I should have called later."

She could hear Ellie breathe for a moment, as if deciding whether or not to hang up.

Finally Ellie asked almost coolly, "How have you been, Ruth?"

"David's dead," Ruth blurted out, mentally cursing herself for her lack of tact.

"I'm sorry to hear that. Was it sudden?"

"Animal attack." Ruth choked out a laugh. "Just a bear. A little old momma bear."

"Wow...that's so strange. I'm so sorry. Are you okay?" Ellie asked.

"I'm okay," Ruth lied.

Ellie hesitated before asking, "Is there anyone you can talk to there?"

Ruth replied, "No....no not really."

Ellie sighed. "You can't phone me like this anymore, Ruth. We both agreed..."

Ruth smiled weakly. "I know. I know. I just wanted to hear a friendly voice, that's all. It's hard doing this alone. I'm still getting used to it."

Ellie paused before saying softly, "Me too. Rue... I don't want to come off as an asshole. I just... If we keep doing this, then neither of us can really get any closure. We both agreed. Rue..."

"I know," Ruth admitted, "I just... You know what, I'm okay. I really am. Listen, I'm going to be staying here a little longer than I originally thought. But when I get back...maybe we could just have coffee or something."

Ruth could imagine a smile as Ellie replied, "I'd like that. Rue..."

"I know," Ruth said gently. "It's okay."

"I was half worried you wanted to get back together now that he's dead," Ellie admitted. "That's really awful of me. I'm sorry. I really am."

Ruth closed her eyes. "I better let you go. I'll call you when I'm back in town."

Ellie said goodbye and she hung up the phone.

Ruth walked upstairs to her childhood room, sitting on her sister's bed as she glanced out the window at the land across the road. She held her head in her hands as she bent forward and burst into tears.

CHAPTER THREE

R UTH HELD THE PHONE to her cheek as she washed the last of the dirty dishes from the funeral. She listened as her supervisor continued to berate her, watching Cora fall asleep by the still-warm oven.

"Mildred," Ruth cut her off. "You're not telling me anything I haven't told myself. But I have a duty here. They need me. It's not uncommon for students to take time off in cases of family emergencies."

"Ruth, I am sorry your brother died, I really am. But...just don't take too much time. You have all the data at home, you can start forming your argument. But it's difficult supervising you long distance. If you manage to get back by spring, at least we can prepare you for the oral defense."

Ruth smiled weakly. "I promise. In the spring, back at work. I just need time to get things in order here. I'll drop in when I'm in the city next week."

"I'd like that. I'll have a stack of readings for you, just for fun. Take care of yourself, Ruth."

Ruth hung up and drained the sink. She liked Mildred and it was a good thing she did. Anyone else she would have told to go to hell. She dialed the next call to her uncle, hoping that someone might finally be sympathetic to her.

She dried her hands and waited as the phone rang.

On the eighth ring, Trip picked up, blearily asking, "Hello?"

"Trip?" Ruth asked in confusion. "Were you sleeping? It's nearly noon. Never mind. Listen, can you keep the girls another week? I've got to go into Toronto for a few more days and I don't want them here by themselves."

Trip muttered, "What are you talking about? Your mum picked them up last night, didn't she tell you?"

Ruth groaned, hanging up on him as she reached for her coat. She buttoned up as she dialed Mum, braiding her wet hair loosely under her hat. When no one answered, she threw on her boots and grabbed her keys, heading toward the truck. Cora followed her out the door to the truck, barking patiently to be let in.

Ruth sighed, opening the door and letting the dog hop into the seat beside her.

"We're not making a habit of this," she said, starting the engine.

She drove the ten kilometers down the concession until she reached her mother's farm. It was smaller, really just a bungalow on a six-acre property. She parked her truck in the driveway beside Mum's and knocked on her door. When no one answered, she unlocked it herself and stepped inside.

"Mum," she called out, looking around. "I know you're home. Where are you?"

Her mother walked down the stairs slowly, holding together her white bathrobe with one hand, her hand lingering on the railing as if she were descending into a ballroom.

"Are the girls at school?" Ruth asked.

"No, they're still in bed," Mum replied. "We were all up rather late last night and then with the snow this morning, I didn't think it was safe enough to go out. None of us felt well enough to travel."

Ruth stomped up the stairs. "Esther! Naomi! Get your asses out here. I'm driving you to school. You can still catch the afternoon classes if we leave now."

Mum retreated into the living room, nestling back into her pile of blankets. She sat, the TV playing on mute, as Ruth walked past, finding her sisters asleep on the floor of a darkened room. They stirred as she turned on the light and opened the blinds.

"Get your things," she said. "You're going back to Trip's. But first, you're going to school. I'll pick you something up at Timmy's if you move now."

The teens agreed silently, moving about sleepily to get ready for the day. Ruth re-entered the living room, turning to address her mother.

Mum accused, "It's unnatural the way you are. You expect us to just pick everything back up again as if he were never here. Well, he was. He held this family together after your father died. He was here for us, every day, and he never disappointed me. You left us, Ruth. You abandoned us. These are my children, his sisters; they are allowed to mourn. Some of us have hearts, you soulless—"

Ruth insisted, "If you want to self-destruct, fine, but don't you dare take them down with you. I'm not letting you do this again."

Mum looked at her, eyes bloodshot. "David was right. You really are a bitch."

Ruth said nothing but left the house and waited in the truck for her sisters. They arrived soon after, complaining about their appearances as Ruth started the engine again.

She glanced back in the rearview mirror. "I'm going to be in Toronto a few days next week. You can come with me to Toronto then, but you're staying at Trip's for a while. There's a bear loose in our area. I saw what it did to the fence and it ain't pretty. I'd feel safer if you were closer to Owen Sound."

They agreed, chatting about what they would buy in Toronto. Ruth wanted to ask them what had happened the night before, but she could imagine. She had been close to Esther's age when her father died. She remembered what it was like. Her mother drunk into a stupor, and only David there...and...

The sensation trickled through her body and she gripped the steering wheel. She focused on the road ahead, counting each stripe of the divider until she could catch her breath again. Five seconds in. Seven seconds out.

Ruth arrived back at the farmhouse to see a light blinking on the answering machine. She hit the playback button, taking off her winter gear as the message played.

"This message is for Ruth MacGowan. Ruth, this is Constable Henley. We've found another man like we found your brother, just a few kilometers away down on Concession 15. There's another farmer gone missing too. We're going to post a note about animal attacks in the area. I'm sending a buddy of mine down to fix that fence for you and add in some lighting. I suggest you keep your animals indoors for now and don't go out at night. Just keep clear of the woods for now. Phone me back if you see anything else. Bye for now."

Ruth stood, glancing up at the rifle above the kitchen door. She thought of David under the sheet, his dead white eyes as they covered his face.

She said to Cora, "I guess I'd better buy some more ammo."

Ruth drove into town again. She picked up a few things at the grocery store and went to the bait and tackle shop. She had written down the exact make, model and caliber of the gun, worried that if she got the wrong thing, she would lose the respect of the owner. There was only one spot licensed to sell arms in the town; she didn't want him to think she was an idiot.

She glanced down at her sheet of paper, muttering the details over and over until she had it memorized. She left the truck, undoing her coat before going into the store. She nodded at another farmer before going to the counter.

She opened her mouth to speak, but the cashier shushed her, turning the radio louder.

"Police say Wilson was found three kilometers from the last attack, making this the third attack this week. Residents are asked to remain indoors after nightfall until the animal is captured. If anyone sees any signs of bear activity, they are to phone Officer Kenneth Henley at 519—"

The cashier turned the radio off.

"Shit," he murmured. "I always liked Henry. Good kid. He used to play hockey with my boy after school. Kid couldn't handle a stick even if it was taped to his glove."

"They found him dead?" Ruth asked.

"Yeah." He nodded. "Say he was torn to pieces. Shit, you're one of the MacGowan girls, aren't you. You look enough like your pa. I'm sorry. I guess you're in the right place. If you see that thing, you shoot it dead between the eyes like your papa taught you."

It was David who had taught her to shoot, but she didn't correct him. Their hometown had its right to collective memories and grief.

It was near nightfall when she returned to the farmhouse. Cora greeted her at the door and Ruth knelt down to scratch behind her ear. She went into the kitchen, warming her dinner up again in the oven: a nut loaf she had made earlier. Ruth smiled softly. Even though she and Ellie had broken up months ago, she still couldn't quite get back into the habit of eating meat again.

She threw a hunk to Cora who sniffed and rejected it, going back over to her mat by the door. Ruth bent her head in quiet reflection, praying before tucking in. She ate slowly, enjoying the meal as she thought of what to do next. There were more phone calls...always more phone calls. Her lease would have to be terminated in Toronto if she decided to stay at the farm, and she would have to talk to the dean. And probably other people. Running away from your life took a lot of logistics.

Her thoughts were interrupted by Cora's whining and pawing at the door.

"Can't let you out, girl," Ruth said. "You heard the constable. I don't want to have to bury you beside David."

Cora insisted with a loud bark and Ruth heard panicked groans from the cows. She grabbed her coat, bundling up before taking the gun and heading outside.

The snow was coming down heavily as Ruth made her way to the fence, holding out a flashlight to try to see the path ahead. The light near blinded her, reflecting off the snow.

Ruth heard the animals quiet and she turned off the flashlight, attempting to see past the barn. She saw a figure dart across the snow and she turned the light back on, shouting, "Hey!"

She chased it through the snow, holding her gun the best she could as she reached the last place she had seen the shadow. She looked down and saw the tread of someone barefoot. She turned off her flashlight and held the gun up as she walked forward toward the tree line.

"I see you," Ruth called out, her eyes slowly adjusting. "The woods aren't safe right now. I want to help you, but you need to come forward right now. You'll catch your death out there."

Ruth saw nothing again until she reached the fence. The snow was coming down so heavily she could no longer make out the trail. She made her way back to the house, feeling her way to the barn. Three goats, two cows. All were in order, all seemed to be calm and resting. In the chicken coop she found the same. All accounted for, none distressed.

Whatever it was, if it had been anything at all, was gone.

Ruth returned to the farmhouse and took off her gear, laying it to dry across the kitchen chairs. She hung the gun back up and went upstairs, calling the dog to follow her.

She climbed into the bed and patted the bedding beside her. Cora jumped up, curling under her arm.

"I know I should go back downstairs and brush my teeth," she confided, "but... I don't feel great. I've just had the strangest feelin g...though I guess now I'm talking to the dog, so my mental health might just be shot anyway."

She rolled her eyes as the dog licked her nose.

She reached out, hesitating before turning off the light.

Lying in the dark, she thought of Ellie. One day the previous summer, down by Ontario Place. They were at the Ex. She had spent all afternoon shooting down fixed targets to win her a...what was it now? It had been this strange pink fluffy thing. Ruth couldn't understand why Ellie wanted to bring that thing home with her then, but she didn't care. She would do anything for Ellie.

As she slipped into her dreams, the targets shifted, each becoming the buck in the forest, each looking her dead in the eye as David slipped his finger over hers, coaxing her to pull the trigger.

CHAPTER FOUR

T HE ALARM WOKE HER and she startled, accidently kicking the dog off the bed. She groaned, smelling her own breath. She made her way downstairs in the dark, putting on the coffee pot before getting dressed.

There were more arrangements to make, but the animals needed to be fed first. It was near six when she returned to the house, fresh milk in a bucket, fresh eggs in the carton. She washed them and put them in the refrigerator before making herself oatmeal.

When she was finished eating and was washing the dishes, she saw a truck pull into the driveway. She went out and met the handyman, who shook her hand only briefly before moving his truck and supplies farther back into the property.

She went to her usual step, drinking coffee on the back porch as Cora sat protectively by her side. She thought of the events of the night before. The snow had covered any trace now, buried what had happened deep below.

If anything had really happened at all.

She abandoned her cup of coffee and went inside, the dog following faithfully behind her. She'd go back to Toronto early. She needed to get out of that house.

As Ruth unlocked the apartment door, the last thing she was expecting to see was Ellie turning around to face her. Esther and Naomi leaned in to see as Ruth entered.

"What the hell are you doing here?" Ruth asked, shocked.

Ellie apologized, "You said you were going away for a few days and I still had my key. I left some books here and one of my journals. I was typing up my notes when I noticed some of my work from a few months ago was missing. I should have called to let you know; I'm sorry, but I thought you were out of town. I was just going to lock it and slide my key under the door, I swear. Are these...are these your sisters?"

Ruth paused and said slowly, "Yes. Esther, Naomi, this is my...this is Ellie."

Ellie smiled sadly. "I've heard so much about you both. I'm sorry, I didn't mean to spoil your time in the city. I've got what I needed, I'll head out."

Ellie paused before handing over the key, folding her fingers over Ruth's hand before letting go.

"I'm sorry," she said quietly and Ruth closed her fist around the key.

"You better go," Ruth said and Ellie nodded, leaving without another word.

Ruth closed the door and then turned, seeing Esther's blush and Naomi's smirk.

Naomi commented, "She's hot. Didn't think you could pull off someone that hot."

Esther blushed deeper and Ruth rolled her eyes.

"Enough you two," she said. "Now there's a pullout couch; you two can stay there. If you don't mind doing some packing at night, you can do what you like during the day if you keep your cell phones on. I'm going to be studying, but you can stay up as long as you like so long as your homework gets done. Any questions?"

Naomi asked, "Why did you guys break up? She seems really into you."

Esther flushed further before excusing herself from the room.

Ruth frowned, watching her sister leave before saying, "Sometimes these things just don't work out, that's all. You go settle in. I'll take you out for dinner. There's a really nice Thai place around the corner."

Naomi went to unpack her backpack and Ruth went into the bedroom, seeing Esther on her phone. She could tell from the tone in her voice that she was talking to Mum.

"I've got to call you back," Esther said quietly, glancing at Ruth.

"Everything okay?" Ruth asked as she hung up the phone.

"Fine." Esther smiled faintly.

Ruth nodded. "Come on then. Go freshen up and we'll grab some dinner."

They returned from the restaurant, leftovers in tow, Naomi chattering away cheerfully.

"I love this place!" she cheered gleefully. "Can we go clubbing? I'll even go to a lesbian bar; it would be so much fun."

Esther paled and Ruth replied, "When you're nineteen, I'll take you, though you're going to find it's nothing too exciting. Or maybe you'll be a bigger partier than me. When I moved to the village, I stuck mainly to the sports bars and the library."

"Then how do you meet people?" Naomi asked.

"Everywhere, like most folks do," Ruth teased. "I met Ellie at school, boring enough as that is. The last two before her I met at work. I think you think life in the big city is much more glamorous and exciting then it actually is."

"So you've...dated other women?" Esther asked quietly.

Ruth grabbed the takeout bags and put them in the fridge. "A few. Only two big relationships, a few others casually. Nothing to brag about."

"Did you love them?" Esther asked.

Ruth frowned as she tried to rearrange the fridge to accommodate the remnants of dinner. "I guess so. I guess I always figured love would be different when you're with the right person but while it lasted, it was love. But...yeah. I loved Ellie, at least."

"So why did you break up then?" Naomi asked.

Ruth forced a smile as she returned to the living room. "It doesn't matter. Now come on. I'm sure your love lives are more exciting than mine. I've got some chips and salsa. Let's stay up talking about boys and braiding each other's hair."

Naomi laughed and Esther smiled a little more earnestly.

Hours later when Naomi had passed out asleep and Ruth was heading toward her own bed, Esther stopped her, holding onto her sister's arm.

"Rue," Esther said quietly. "I... I want to say..."

Ruth knelt down in front of her sister as she sat at the edge of the pullout bed.

Ruth said softly, "It's okay. You spent the last six years living with David. You've had plenty of time to hear from him and Mum how I've made terrible choices in my life. But the thing is, I'm happy. Even now, even with all this shit going on in our lives. I'm living the life I want. I know you love me and you're struggling right now. That's okay. You're trying and that's all that matters to me."

Esther hugged her, burying her face in Ruth's hair. She held onto her as if she was still small. Ruth could remember when Esther was just four, crawling into bed with her on stormy nights, her pigtails trailing after her when she ran.

Esther whispered, "I'm so sorry."

"Me too," Ruth said quietly. "I love you. You know that. Come on, you should get some rest."

Esther pulled away, nodding. Ruth kissed her on the forehead, fighting the urge to tuck her in like she had done when her sister was small.

Ruth went into her room and flopped down on her bed. It still smelled like Ellie. It shouldn't. She had been gone for weeks now, but Ruth had forgotten what her apartment smelled like. She forgot the lingering spice in the kitchen, the scent of coconut oil and shea butter on their sheets. It smelled like home. She wondered how long it would take until the apartment held only the stink of her own dirty dishes and used sweatpants.

Hearing a chime, Ruth took out her phone to see a text from Ellie, once again apologizing for intruding.

Ruth was tempted to ask her to come back to the farm with her, to finally meet her family, but how would she even explain everything Ellie was to her? Everything she had been? No. Ellie was moving on. She had her own wants, her own projects, her own dreams. Ellie was finally becoming herself again, her life flourishing without Ruth in it. The best thing that Ruth could do was to let her live it.

It was dark when Ruth pulled back into the driveway. It felt as if she had been gone for another lifetime. For two days, she had kept it together. The girls were mourning their brother; they didn't need to know how badly screwed up their big sister was.

The girls were safely at Trip's now. The snow had melted down a little, becoming icy as it froze over again. It shone underneath the full moon and Ruth was careful as she walked back across it, carrying the dog. Cora acted as if her nights at Trip's had been a burden, whining and crying unless Ruth paid attention to her. Ruth expected that the rest of the animals had been much less bothered by her absence, not caring who fed them as long as somebody did. Trip had been over there often enough that they probably preferred his presence anyway.

Ruth went into the house, letting Cora down as she saw the flickering red light on the answering machine. She skipped the first two, hearing her mother's voice, and focused on the third.

"Ruth, this is Constable Henley. I don't know if you've heard, but there's been another killing, just south of your property. You let me know if you've seen anything. Your uncle told me you've been out of town, but if you're back, keep your eyes peeled. I'll try back tomorrow. I suggest you stay out of the woods, even in daylight, until we figure this out."

The wind howled and Ruth turned, glancing at the gun above the kitchen door. She kept her winter gear on, picking the gun up as she went out into the snow. If there was an animal lurking about, she needed to make sure the fence was secure.

The thin ice layer cracked underneath her feet as she walked, first to the now-mended fence, and then to David's grave. She had knelt to clean the snow off his headstone when she saw marks in the ice-crusted snow above the mound. She traced them and frowned. It looked like fingernails, as if someone had been clawing at his grave.

She looked around, but could not see any other signs of a creature or even another person having been there besides her. She picked up the gun again and returned to the house, hanging it back up as she kicked off her boots.

She put out water for the dog and went into the living room. She knelt in front of the fireplace, starting a fire with the box of matches on the mantle. Settling into the nearest chair, she reached for the first book in the pile that Mildred had given her. She had only finished the first short story when she heard a knock at the kitchen door. Frowning, she put the book down before walking into the kitchen and paused before opening the blinds.

Ruth froze when she saw it. As white as the snow, with a light covering of hair on its body, a figure stood naked before her, its pupil-less eyes glancing up at her.

Ruth's initial reaction was to shoot it dead and bury it before any questions could be asked. But instead she opened the door, as if she were following an old script. It wasn't so much a compulsion, but a feeling like she had already rehearsed this moment. This was her role in this scene—one she had played over and over, maybe in another lifetime. She was the one who opened the door, always, so she did it again now. A continuous act of treason against her home, against her family, and against herself. This was a betrayal; one she had been too late to make a conscious decision about committing. Her body had already made the choice for her.

The creature asked in a quiet voice, "Will you let me in?"

Ruth understood this as an invitation. If she turned it away, it would leave her alone and never return to this house. But if she invited it in, she didn't know what would happen next. She didn't remember, if this was indeed all a memory from some other life. Or maybe, like a dream in the first moments after waking, the logic of this scenario was quickly falling apart.

Ruth refused. "No."

"You will want to invite me in, human," it said. "I cannot protect you out here."

"Protect me from what?" Ruth demanded.

"Invite me in and I will tell you."

Ruth grabbed the rifle and stepped back before opening the door. She cocked her gun and kept it fixed on the creature as it walked in.

The being wiped its snow-clad feet on the mat—an oddly human gesture. It glanced around, its long translucent hair reflecting the surroundings, before it walked forward into the living room, staring at the fire. It knelt on the hearth, holding its thin white hand out to touch the flames. It withdrew quickly, its fingers flashing a pink shade of flesh before returning to white.

Ruth lowered her rifle, but only slightly. "Did you kill my brother?"

It shook its head. "No."

"Do you know what did?" Ruth questioned further. "Was it a bear?"

"No," it replied. "It was not."

Ruth glanced over its body. From the slight curves in the waist and the suggestion of breasts beneath the translucent hair, she thought it could almost pass for human, even female.

"What are you?" she asked.

"I am... There is no word in your language for us," it replied. "Nothing that would not name me as a monster. I am...what I am. I am Werros."

It was a pointless question, considering what was standing in front of her, but she couldn't ignore the impulse. "So, you're not human?"

It paused before shaking its head.

Ruth demanded, "Then what are you?"

"A predator," it said, the firelight reflecting in its hair. "We have hunted the forests of this continent since before humanity ever stepped foot on its soil."

"All the dead bodies..." Ruth thought out loud. "Do you hunt humans?"

It paused, then admitted, "We should not."

"What does that mean?"

It stood, its small frame becoming apparent as it glanced up at Ruth, and its violet irises retracted against the pure white of its eyes. Its voice sounded almost like a worn record, its words high and static, with an ambient hum with each breath.

"I have come for the one who hunted your brother and the other three men," it said; "I came for your assistance. It lingers in your territory. You would see me eventually and I know you have seen my tracks by now. I heard your voice. You offered to help me. I did not want to harm you. But I must slay this being and I must do it before more of your people are killed and we are revealed."

"Are you like a vampire or something?" Ruth asked in confusion.

It smiled, its slight fangs glinting in the firelight. "Not as you would understand it. I am not dead; I am a hunter. Your kind has the right to fear us, but...what is happening here is not permitted. I have come to amend the issue before more damage is done."

"What do you want from me?" Ruth asked, gripping the rifle tighter.

"For now," it said, "let me rest here in the daylight. Too many men are out combing the woods, and my skin camouflages me best at night and I am...nocturnal as you might understand it. I will hunt down this outlier. If you keep me out of sight, this menace will be over shortly."

Ruth paused, thinking this over, before asking, "What do I call you?"

It bristled slightly and said, "I have no name that you can safely know. Must you call me something? I do not imagine there will be another Werros in this house."

Ruth said, "Among humans, it is customary to be called by one's name. For instance, my name is Ruth MacGowan. MacGowan is my family name, Ruth refers to me as my own person."

"I know what a name is," it replied, letting out a near chuckle, "but among my kind, it is more complicated than this. But if you must, you can give me a...nickname."

"Well," Ruth asked, "are you...male, female? Other? Both?"

"Biologically," it said, "my kind is mainly female as you would understand it. We possess similar reproductive organs as those of your kind would. But...it is not the same. We have factions, lineages, other ways of understanding our bodies as roles. There are so many with my reproductive organs, it would seem...unhelpful to view us all as female."

They glanced at each other and Ruth flushed, as if only noticing now that the creature was naked.

"Do you wear clothes?" Ruth asked. "If you stay here, there is a chance you'll be seen. Can you blend in?"

It replied, "I have been fasting. When we fast, we appear as we truly are. But if I indulge in human blood, yes, I will appear more human. It is an evolutionary reflex, to better mimic our prey. It would be wise if I broke my fast."

"You want my blood," Ruth stated, anxiety flooding her.

It said quietly, "In the old ways, my people only take blood from the willing. There is...intimacy in the act. Closeness, trust. We need so little to survive. We do not need to take what is not ours. Ours by gift, not by coercion."

Ruth snapped, "If you're so ethical, why did one of you kill my brother?"

"I do not know," it replied, glancing toward the fire again, "but that is why we must be careful. The laws of my kin do not bind her as they should."

It turned back to look at Ruth, its eyes fixating on a point just below her chin. Ruth could almost feel the blood pump faster in her body, coming closer to the skin. Ruth fought the urge to cover her throat.

"You could call me, Mishe," it said quietly. "It is what I was called when I was young. It is a pet name, it will not harm you." Mishe looked away and said, "You will be tired, human. Rest. I will keep your home safe while I search for her. I require little from you, only a place to rest safely. We shall keep each other alive."

Mishe left through the kitchen without another word, walking out into the snow with an odd lightness, its hair shimmering in the moonlight. As it strode, it faded into the wintery world around them. The creature was right. It was damn good camouflage.

Ruth stood in the doorway, listening to the wind howl. Cora whined and she went to the dog's side, scratching her ear.

"Come on, girl," she said quietly.

Ruth had trouble falling asleep, fearing when the creature would return to the house. She grabbed a work knife from the kitchen, keeping it just under her mattress, her fingers mere inches away. Just in case.

CHAPTER FIVE

RUTH WOKE TO THE alarm, grabbing the knife as she reached out. She glanced around. The dog was gone, but otherwise, nothing in the room had changed. She pulled her housecoat around her and went downstairs, putting on the coffee pot before glancing outside.

She wondered if she'd dreamt it all, the night before, but just then she saw the creature in a shimmer as the sun rose across the field. Mishe's face was stern as it walked, its jaw fixed as it went forward, its feet barely touching the ground.

It entered through the back door without knocking and said to Ruth: "Do you have a room that will lock?"

Ruth stood, holding the knife out, her hand shaking. "So you are real."

"As I was last night," Mishe reminded.

Ruth admitted, "I was still hoping otherwise."

Mishe stood still, its nearly blank eyes scanning Ruth's body in assessment, and said, "You have already invited me into your home. Are you rescinding your offer?"

Ruth hesitated, watching the creature standing in her kitchen.

Mishe reminded her, "I have been here in your forest for days and not harmed you. I would be foolish to do so at this point. Now. Do you have a room that locks?"

Ruth nodded, lowering the knife as she gripped it harder. "Third on the right upstairs."

"When you are finished attending your charges, come and find me. We have many things to discuss."

Ruth dressed quickly and went out to the chicken coop, collecting eggs and feeding her birds. All accounted for, none flustered or angry. She took this as a good sign as she picked up the basket of eggs and went to the barn.

She opened the door and screamed.

A man lay dead on the ground, his expression blank. His chest was torn, his organs splayed across the ground, his heart bearing the marks of something with large teeth. The cows were terribly upset, bellowing out as if for help and keeping as far as they could from it. The goats were equally uneasy in their stall, panicking at the sound of their barn mates in distress.

Ruth ran back into the house, grabbing the phone. She shrieked as she felt someone pull it from her hands.

"So you have found him," Mishe said, putting the phone back down.

Ruth accused it fearfully. "What did you do? How—what? I need to phone the police. Did you put him there? Did you kill him?"

Mishe shook its head. "I tried to save his life."

Ruth growled, "I don't believe you. I'm phoning the cops."

"Do so. But will they not wonder how he ended up on your property?"

"You're blackmailing me."

"I'm stating a fact," Mishe replied. "Let me explain what has happened and then you can phone your officer if you wish."

"You've got two minutes," Ruth said.

Mishe explained quickly, "I found him in the road just after midnight. She was standing over him. We...we do not eat flesh. We drink blood. It is all we need to survive. But she was already tearing through his chest with her teeth I tried to fight her off, but she cut me. We cannot lose blood. We have so little and we need every drop to survive. I fell and she devoured his heart. I brought him back here once she was finished, to hide the body and for his people to mark his death."

Ruth paused, looking down at the gash across its chest and said, "You're hurt."

Mishe said, "I need rest. It will heal in time, but I need rest...and blood. It need not be human or fresh. I will hunt when I am better."

Mishe stepped forth, its knees shaking as it tried to climb the stairs. Instinctively, Ruth picked it up and carried it into David's former bedroom. She turned on the lights and laid Mishe in the bed.

Mishe closed its eyes, its breathing rattled and slow.

Ruth sat on the bed and muttered, "So much for keeping me safe, huh?"

She was startled as the creature laughed, cold and hollow in its chest. "Yes. I could not even protect myself. It has been a long time since I fought one of my kind. I forgot how sharp our teeth are."

Ruth looked down at the jagged cut. It did not bleed, but it was deep, nearly to the bone. Or at least, she guessed. Who knew if these things even had bones; maybe they were all cartilage like a shark or something else equally aquatic and terrifying.

Mishe said weakly, "I will be better by evening. Let me rest, human. There will be more time to explain later."

"I'm going to phone the police," Ruth said. "The guy's family needs to be notified. I'll tell them I found him on the edge of the property and brought him into the barn to keep the body safe from predators. No need to mention any monsters."

"I appreciate your deception," Mishe murmured, its eyes closing.

Ruth paused in morbid curiosity as the creature lay in her dead brother's bed. When she saw the rise and fall of its chest, she left the room.

She pulled out her cell phone and dialed the police station.

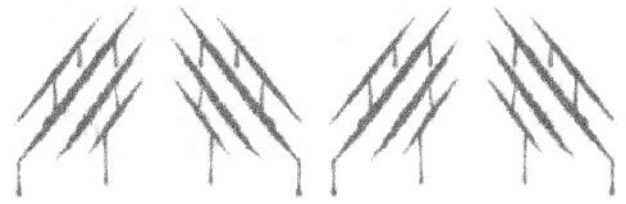

Henley questioned, "You get any shots off at the thing?"

Ruth said truthfully, "Didn't see it at all. He must have died during the night."

Henley sighed. "Damn bear. We'll get it yet."

Ruth watched them cart the body away. When the police were gone, the evidence collected and photographed, she glanced upward, toward David's bedroom window. She saw the curtains flutter as a hand retracted from view.

She made her way upstairs, unlocking the bedroom door. Mishe lay again on the bed, its marks healing remarkably quickly. Its hair splayed out around it, reflecting the blue of the painted wall.

"You don't do a very good job of hiding," Ruth remarked angrily.

"I wanted to see the police officers," Mishe said. "Though I cannot see much in the day. It is too bright, even this early."

Mishe looked even more fragile then, like a broken doll. Ruth's heart softened.

Ruth sighed. "Be more careful."

She turned to leave and Mishe asked, "Do you miss him?"

Ruth said nothing.

Mishe continued, "The first time I saw you was out there in the snow. You were talking to him when he wasn't there. You seemed so...angry. I was intrigued. I thought to go to you for help. You lived alone and you were so angry. You were a human who can be alone. That is something admirable among my kind, something desirable. But it is still natural to mourn the dead."

Ruth murmured, "I don't miss him. I can't get away from him."

Ruth left the room, not waiting for Mishe to reply.

Ruth woke from her armchair, hearing her name croaked from the upper level. Ruth went up the stairs slowly, unlocking the door to see Mishe on the floor, the blankets strewn around it as it tried to stand.

Mishe murmured feverishly, "I need blood. I need...I can't..."

"I've got some raw liver in the freezer," Ruth said. "I can thaw it out...or is frozen okay?"

Mishe nodded deliriously. "Yes...yes...please. Frozen."

Ruth ran down to the cellar, grabbing a few pieces of meat and bundling them in her housecoat to protect her hands. She ran back up to Mishe and laid them out.

The Werros glanced up and said, "You may not want to watch this."

"Can't be worse than anything I've seen," Ruth chuckled. "You forget I grew up on a farm. My people are notorious for having strong stomachs."

Mishe frowned and picked up a piece of the frozen meat, its fingers tearing it apart like bread. It bit into it, teeth flashing. It sucked, draining the meat of its colour, peeling it apart to break through the blood vessels. It shucked the rest to the side and went to the next piece of meat. It would be difficult to say that the colour had returned to its face, but its hands stopped trembling, its eyes grew more focused. The cut on its chest paled, patching together until there was a dull scar on its white skin.

It looked up, blood smearing down its chin, eyes pinned on Ruth.

"Thank you," Mishe murmured. "Thank you." The creature picked itself up and said, "It was foolish of me not to break my fast before I tried to find her. You have kept me safe, human. That is more than I have done for you."

Ruth hesitated. "You're welcome."

It was near evening when Mishe descended the stairs, draped in the bed sheets— and suddenly, Ruth started questioning whether or not she should be referring to Mishe as "it." Ruth had once gone out with an enby who used "it" for itself, but that didn't feel right here. Ruth had been viewing Mishe as a creature, calling it "it" like she'd call a wild animal from a distance, not as a fellow human being who had reclaimed the term for itself. Maybe "she" was kinder for now, even if Mishe claimed that any femininity she had was irrelevant.

The creature's footsteps made no sound on the creaky steps. Ruth watched her as she made her way into the living space, tentatively, as if any piece of the ground might rise up and shatter her in two.

The Werros said quietly, "Would you find something for me to wear when I return?"

"You'll hunt naked?" Ruth asked skeptically.

"I do not feel the cold as you do," she said quietly. "Wearing clothing would only slow me down and make me visible to those seeking me."

"Where will you go tonight?" Ruth asked.

"Farther east," she replied, folding the sheet before dropping it to the floor. "There is a wooded area on your neighbours' property. I will search for her there."

"Do you know her?" Ruth asked. "I mean, did you recognize her?"

"My kind is solitary outside our kin," Mishe replied. "No. No, I did not recognize her. It is likely we have never met."

She went to the kitchen door, watching the sunset with anticipation. Ruth stood beside her, watching the snow drift across the fields.

Ruth asked, "What can I to do to help?"

Mishe replied, "You need rest, human. The night is my world, not yours."

She touched Ruth's arm in an approximation of affection before she left, fading into the snowy woods.

Ruth went back into the living room, pausing as the phone rang.

She picked it up. "Hello?"

Esther said, "Hi sis."

Ruth's hand went to her forehead. In all of this, she had forgotten what lay outside the house. Her sisters, her mother...they were all still grieving while she had apparently invited an ancient monster to make itself at home. What had she even done that day? Where had the time even gone?

"How are you?" Ruth asked.

Esther replied, "I'm worried about Mum. She hasn't phoned us since we got back from Toronto. I tried texting her and everything. I'm just worried."

"I'll drive by her place tomorrow if she hasn't responded by then," Ruth promised. "I'm sure she's fine."

"I just feel guilty leaving her there by herself," Esther said. "I... I can't imagine what she's going through. I just... I don't know if she can do this on her own."

Ruth thought of the days after her father's death, of her mother lying on the couch, barely moving, barely breathing, her hands running over his photo, the bottle of wine on the ground. Whenever Ruth tried to move the bottle, her mother would sit up, her blood-red eyes meeting hers like a wild animal's. Ruth would flee as her mother screamed for her father and wailed for hours once more.

"She's survived this once," Ruth said. "She's tougher than you give her credit for. Look... Esther..."

Ruth sat down, holding the receiver close as she said softly, "I was just a little younger than you are now when Dad died. God, you were so small then. Barely two, just a baby. I can still see that little girl in your face, especially when you smile. I know you don't remember those days, but I do. Mum took care of you. She pushed through everything to make sure she could be there for you."

"Rue," Esther confessed. "I *know*. I know you basically raised the two of us, you and David both. I remember *you* being at soccer games, not Mum. You made our lunches and picked us up from school when we were sick. When I broke my arm, you were the one to take me to the hospital because Mum was crying too hard. Or that's what you told me then, because you didn't want me to know she'd started drinking again. You took care of us, you and David, and I... I really, really miss him. Since he's been gone, I'm just... Rue, I'm so scared. Mum needs me and I don't know how to help her."

"Esther, baby," Ruth murmured, feeling tears run down her face. "You listen to me. You listen to me for once, okay? I know you want to take care of her. I know you think you can save her, keep all of us together. I know... I understand that temptation. I know you've got a soft heart. I want you to keep it soft. I gave up a lot of things for the both of you and I don't regret it, but I shouldn't have had to take care of you two. It wasn't my job and this isn't yours. I... I don't want you to take care of her. That sounds harsh and awful, but I want you to have a childhood and grow up not having to worry about everyone else. It'll just wear you out and you're too young, baby, you're too young for this shit. None of this weight belongs to you."

Ruth could hear Esther crying on the other end of the phone.

Ruth asked, "Are you okay? Do you need me to come over?"

Esther said, muffled, "No... I just... I really missed you. And I really miss David. I miss... I miss when we used to all be together. I miss it. It was so good then; it was perfect. I don't know why you had to go away. It would have been okay if you stayed. We would have understood about you being...you know."

Ruth hesitated before saying, "I know. It's hard. But we're going to get through this. You lean on me and your sister, okay? You're going to survive this."

She swore she could hear her sister smile as Esther said, "I know."

"I love you," Ruth said quietly, "I love you both so much."

Esther said, "I love you too."

Ruth remembered the wild thing hunting in her yard and said, "I better go. I gotta make sure the barn is locked up."

"You shouldn't go out after dark," Esther reminded her. "I heard about the guy in the barn from Uncle Trip... That's really awful. I can't imagine."

"I'll be okay," Ruth promised; "I'll be fine. You go text some cute boy or whatever you kids do."

Esther chuckled. "Okay. Bye Ruth."

Ruth lowered the receiver, clicking the phone off before putting it back in the charger. Cora whined from across the room and Ruth whistled for the dog to come over.

Cora jumped into her lap and curled in, resting her head on Ruth's knee. Ruth relaxed into the chair, petting the dog before picking up her book again. She flipped to the right page and started to read.

She scratched behind Cora's ear and said, "Should I read aloud to you? I used to do that for the girls when they were little."

She flipped the page just as the crack of a gunshot sounded through the house. Cora jumped up, barking furiously. Ruth stood up and dashed to the kitchen, pulling on her coat and scarf before grabbing her own weapon and shoving her feet into her boots. running out into the cold night.

She looked around, running into the field with the dog behind her. Ruth headed toward the forests, arriving at the recently fixed fence. She heard a scream and she climbed the fence, abandoning the dog on the other side as Cora howled. She ran forward, following the scream as she moved carefully across the frozen river, gun straight ahead as she scanned the ground.

She saw the man crawling toward her in the snow, his bloodied foot dragging behind him as he reached out to her. She raced to his side, kneeling to check his wound.

"Ruth? Is that you?" the man asked woozily. "I remember your brother... That thing...that thing is still out there... Oh God... Oh God..."

"It's okay," Ruth said as calmly as she could. "Keep still, I'm going to tie this off. My property's less than two klicks away. I'll carry you if I have to."

"You won't be fast enough," he groaned. "That thing, I barely got away from it. It's not a bear, Ruth. God, I don't know what it is, but it's not a bear."

"I know," Ruth assured him, "I know. I'm going to get you out of here, okay?"

Ruth tied off the wound with her scarf, helping him to his feet. She brought his arm over her shoulder, carrying him the best she could as they hobbled toward the fence.

They barely made it six feet before she felt the blow to her head. She yelped as she rolled forward, the man thrown off her back. She staggered to her feet, her head ringing as she reached for her gun.

A Werros snarled up at her, its teeth glinting in the dark. It leaped at Ruth, knocking her to the ground. She was pinned as the creature's teeth lingered inches from her face.

It smelled her skin and grinned. "You're female. I thought you were a man, all tall and stocky as you are."

It put its hands around her throat, whispering in her ear, "Too bad. You would have been so delicious, just as tasty as your brother."

Its teeth grazed her cheek as it choked her. Ruth arched her back, trying not to black out as she reached for her gun. Then it struck, biting her around her jawbone. Ruth froze, her heart racing as she felt what must have been some kind of poison ebb into her veins. She tried to cry out, fingers reaching and grasping nothing but snow as her eyes grew heavier, the creature leaving her alone to fatally embrace the man. He screamed as it split open his chest. Ruth watched in silent horror, lacking the air needed to even whimper.

She fought to stay conscious as she saw another creature dart into her field of vision, knocking the predator off its feet. They fought, snarling and hissing as they tore at each other. Ruth managed to finally put her fingers around the barrel of her gun and got herself upright enough to shoot. She hit one, the other flying off into the woods.

The injured creature loped toward her, holding its side as Ruth dropped the gun, her hands growing numb. She whimpered as it arrived at her side, its expression softening...becoming almost human as it picked her up.

"It's you," Ruth murmured as she slipped into the black. "Sorry, sorry, I'm sorry."

CHAPTER SIX

"Ruth... Ruth you must keep awake. The poison must be expelled. You will die, human. You need to keep your eyes open."

Ruth frowned as she stirred, recognizing her bedding strewn around her. She smelled vomit, blood, and shit, and she fought the urge to hurl onto the floor.

"Don't fight your instincts," the Werros instructed, her cold hands touching Ruth's neck. "You must get rid of the poison."

Ruth vomited, her stomach heaving until there was nothing left. She felt her eyes closing as her body shuddered. The black hit her just as the nausea rose again.

She smelled the room as she woke and nearly retched again. She stumbled into the bathroom, washing her chest and neck. Her fingers gingerly touched her bruised jawline, tracing over the marks of teeth.

"Mishe," she groaned.

She made her way into David's bedroom and saw the creature lying on the floor, blood crusted now into the carpet. There was a wound, a bullet hole clean through her body, pulsing with her breathing. She moaned quietly, her fingers digging into the carpet.

Ruth knelt beside her and asked, "What can I do? What can I do?"

The creature's eyes were nearly glazed over as she asked, "I need blood."

Without thinking, Ruth held out her hand. "Then take it."

Mishe hesitated only an instant before leaning forth, her teeth sinking into Ruth's flesh. Ruth expected it to hurt, but she felt as if a needle had poked her and she was only very slowly bleeding into it. Like blood was being drawn from her and replaced with something sickly and syrupy, so black and thick she could almost taste it. Ruth's head fell back as memory flowed into her like an IV drip, spreading up her arm from the point of penetration.

David was standing above her, his belt in his hand, that look of disgust in his eyes. She was here in this same room, cowering and whimpering. She had tried so hard not to cry. She didn't want the girls to hear her, didn't want to risk the violence seeping out from under the door.

Then David kneeled beside her, cupping her chin as their eyes met. Ruth wanted to scream at him, she wanted to remind him, to remind the whole universe that he was dead. He could not touch her anymore. He could not hurt her ever again.

She threw him across the room as the memory broke and she saw the Werros flung from her, her blood trickling down Mishe's chin.

Mishe wiped her mouth and apologized. "I am sorry if I have harmed you."

"What was that?" Ruth gasped.

"It is a trick, nothing more. My kind's bite can inflict visions, hallucinations. Memories, sometimes, but only those which are already close to the surface. The ones you need no help to recall."

Ruth held her wrist in her hand, feeling the skin heal under her fingers. She looked up and saw Mishe stand. Her skin was darker now, almost a faint pink underneath her icy complexion. Her hair had colour too now, white as snow itself, no longer translucent. Her eyes had softened, black pupils emerging through the surface of her violet irises.

Ruth froze, her eyes glancing down at the rest of her. Mishe's body hair had darkened as well; her breasts were now fuller, her lips wider and softer.

Mishe said, "I am still the creature you shot in the forest. I am merely in better disguise now."

"This is what you look like...when...you are human?"

"I am never human," Mishe corrected. "My body simply adapts. I will return to my familiar form in a few days unless I drink more from you or another human."

"I'm sorry," Ruth replied, unsure of what else to say.

Mishe stated, "I try to abstain. It is...the best kindness I can give. But I have been foolish twice now. This being is faster than I, stronger than I. I think it is because it has fed so much. It will only grow stronger."

Ruth watched her walk across the room, the bullet hole a mere scar.

"Please," Mishe said. "I grow a bit cooler now. Would you give me something to wear?"

Ruth stood and walked into her disgusting room with the Werros in quiet step behind her.

"You're much smaller than me," Ruth apologized, "but I have some pants, and we can hem them for you. And a few work shirts."

Mishe bowed upon receiving the clothes. She left without speaking.

Ruth had either thrown out or washed everything she had vomited on by mid morning. The morning chores were done on an empty stomach, and she felt nauseous from the forced coffee. Ruth now sat in the kitchen, eating her eggs and toast as the Werros walked down the stairs.

Cora growled as the Werros entered the space.

Mishe explained, "I smell like a predator to her."

She sat in the chair beside Ruth, her clothes making Mishe look even smaller as she glanced around, avoiding Ruth's eyes.

"What happened last night?" Ruth asked.

The creature replied, "You were poisoned. Our bite can harm others as you have no doubt realized by this morning. I controlled it since I was not trying to harm you. In certain doses, it can stop a human heart. I was hunting when I saw her in the forest. She was eating the male and I attacked her. I thought she would be vulnerable then. I thought I had her."

"And then I shot you. Sorry about that."

Mishe shook her head. "You were attempting to defend yourself. The shot perhaps saved us both. The distraction allowed it to escape instead of killing me first. When I saw that you were alive, I took you back here. Your body expelled most of the poison on its own. I believe you were unconscious, but you occasionally spoke. You were calling for a woman. Ellie. I think you thought you were dying. When I knew you were out of danger, I left. I was growing weaker and needed rest to heal. I would have died if you had not helped me."

"It seems only right," Ruth stated.

A faint smile crossed Mishe's lips.

Ruth paused. "Listen... Why didn't she eat me? I mean, she was obviously trying to kill me, but she didn't drink my blood. Why would she just leave me—wait, let's back up a sec. You called her 'she' before and 'it' now. Which should I be using for you two?"

"Either is fine. In our language, there is no distinction. I know in your language, 'it' is considered derogatory to many, but it does not matter in our tongue. Use whatever feels most comfortable to you."

"Thanks, but you didn't answer my other question."

The Werros frowned. "I do not know. It puzzles me. She is at-tracted to this spot and has killed many. Our kind... It would be a gorge to drink so much blood in such a short period of time, a frenzied feast without purpose. Yet you would have been dead by the time she had drained that man. We do not drink from the dead unless we have to...though she is such a puzzle, perhaps she prefers it."

Ruth remembered something suddenly. "She said she was disap-pointed I was female. She said she thought I was male and it was too bad because I would have tasted better."

Mishe said quietly, "She's only attacked men."

Ruth nodded. "As far as I know. Why?"

Mishe said quickly, "There is something I must tell you. There is much to explain, but there is so little time—"

The doorbell rang and they exchanged a look.

"I'll ignore it," Ruth said.

"It would arouse suspicion," the Werros said. "Answer it. I will be upstairs. Be quick, human."

The doorbell rang again as Mishe raced up the stairs. Ruth an-swered the door, only to see her mother on the other side.

"Can I come in?" she asked.

Ruth hesitated, looking around briefly. "The place is a mess, re-ally. I've been having this twenty-four-hour bug, and it's pretty bad. I really don't think you want to come in right now; it's disgusting."

"I changed your diapers," she reminded Ruth. "I can deal with a few dirty tissues."

Ruth didn't want her to ask any more questions, so she finally sighed and said, "Okay, please, come on in."

Mum stepped inside, closing the door behind her. She sniffed around and said, "It smells...strange in here. Did you put on one of those candles your aunt made me?"

"No," Ruth said. "Just some VapoRub. Don't worry about it. How have you been? Esther was telling me last night she hadn't heard from you in a while. Everything okay?"

"Hmm? Yes, things are just fine, dear. I mean...fine as I can expect, I guess. I mean...my son is dead and my daughter is a pervert, but one can only take what one gets."

Ruth bristled as Mum continued, "Esther tells me you were even living with this one. What was her name again? Emma? Emily?"

Ruth didn't answer.

Mum chuckled. "And you thought it was appropriate to bring my daughters to your little love nest while you continued your 'studies?'"

"There were some things I needed to take care of," Ruth said quietly. "I thought it would be good for them to get a break from here."

"Ah, of course," Mum said. "Being with their mother wasn't healthy for them. Better to stay with you in the big city, where you can read your filthy books and cavort with women without a lick of religion in them. We've needed you here, Ruth, and you've gone off and wasted your life pursuing your own selfish wants."

"I'm getting my Master's degree," Ruth replied, "the thing I put on hold to take care of all of you. It took me ten years to get here, Mum. You couldn't afford to send me to university, so I worked full time while I did my B.A. online. All the while taking care of *your* daughters. Then, when I finally left home at twenty-four, it was only because I couldn't study to become a librarian here. Which, by the way, is probably one of the least evil professions on the planet. Is any of that such a terrible thing? Is that so selfish to want to do? It's a good job, it helps people, and I want to take care of myself."

"Well, you've certainly done that."

"I don't know what you want from me," Ruth said in frustration.

"When God gave me three daughters," Mum said coolly, "I thought I would have three sons-in-law. I would have grandchildren. You would all live in the county; we'd all go to church together on Sundays. Three daughters, all good Christian wives and mothers. But what do I get? My son... My only son is dead. Gone. And you... You dare corrupt my last two children. I only have them now and you dare take them away from me, dare expose them to all that is ungodly. You have always simply taken what you wanted, never thinking of what your family needs. I'm glad you'll never have children, Ruth. You would destroy them."

Ruth felt as if she had been struck and something inside of her snapped in two.

"Get out of my house!" Ruth screamed. "Get the hell out now! I don't want to see you on my property again until it's time to bury you too! Get the hell out before I do it now!"

Mum left in huff, slamming the door behind her.

Ruth fell to her knees, crying hysterically as her hands went to her face.

The Werros came down the stairs. "Are you alright, human?"

"Get the hell back up," Ruth warned, pointing angrily at her. "I don't want to see you right now. You stay right up where you are."

Ruth gasped, the sobs racking her lungs as she tried to regain her breath. She rose slowly, grasping onto the table as she brought herself back up to her feet.

She turned, seeing the creature walk toward her.

"What did I just say?" Ruth snarled as Mishe stood before her.

"Trust me," she murmured and bit into her neck.

Ruth let out a muffled scream as she fell to her knees, her vision going black.

Yet the pain subsided and she saw Ellie lying in a hospital bed, grinning sleepily as Ruth lay beside her. Curled into her arms, the tiny baby opened its eyes blearily. A lovely shade of deep brown, just like Ellie's. Little tuffs of hair already, a beautiful complexion. It reminded Ruth of tea with just a splash of milk, the way both she and Ellie drank it every morning together, as if each cup had been a small promise of the future.

"She has your nose," Ellie teased, tears running down her face.

Ruth laughed. "And my ears. Poor thing."

Ellie smiled and pressed her forehead against Ruth's.

"I never thought I could be so happy," she whispered.

Ruth cupped her face, kissing her lightly before taking the infant into her arms. The child nestled into her chest and she held it close, smelling the top of its head.

Ruth knew it wasn't real, but as she held the child to her chest, she wanted to kiss it again and again and promise it that she could keep them safe, all of them safe.

She felt the vision fading and she begged, "No, just another minute, please, please. Please, don't take this away."

She saw the living room as the creature stepped back, watching her face as Ruth came back into the present moment.

Ruth felt the tears streaming down her face and wiped them away. "Can you see what I see?"

"Only a little," Mishe said. "If there was a stronger bond, I would see more. But...I saw the woman. She was the one you were calling for, wasn't she?"

Ruth stood, shaking still. "It doesn't matter now."

"She caused you pain?"

Ruth shook her head. "No... It's more complicated than that... I..."

The Werros looked at her in what appeared to be concern.

Ruth whispered, "I don't know how your kind does things...but among mine, it's not common for two women to end up together. My family didn't approve of her or anyone else before her. I loved her. God... I loved her more than I loved anyone in my life. We were together for two years. I should have married her...though I guess I'm glad I didn't now. It would have been so much messier with lawyers and all of that... I thought I was going to spend the rest of my life with her."

The Werros listened quietly as Ruth continued, sitting down on the couch.

"I wanted a baby. We both did, but I pushed. She wanted to wait a while longer, at least until I was finished with school. We both tried to get pregnant with help from the same clinic, but she took before I did. So I stopped trying. We were happy. God, we were so happy. Then... Then she miscarried five months in. She was ill, I brought her into the hospital... I'll never forget her face when they told us. She didn't talk to me for three days. She just lived as a ghost beside me. We talked about trying again... Well, I did. She thought I was callous, that if it had really been mine, I would have cared more... We fought. It just grew to be too much. Then one day she left. That was about two months ago."

The Werros said nothing, just sat down beside her and listened.

Ruth whispered, "It should have been me. I wish she never had to go through that. I wish it had been me. I never talked to anyone here about any of that. I didn't want to get married because then I would have to tell them. And then hear shit like that—what my mother said. But God... Even if she had known about the baby, I don't think it would have hurt me any worse."

"I'm sorry," Mishe replied quietly.

Ruth sighed and said, "It's okay. It's not... It's not something I should focus on. But thank you...it made it stop hurting, if just for a minute."

"I do not like seeing humans in pain," the creature replied. "Some of my kin might see that as a fault. I do not understand what you have experienced...but I want to say still that I am sorry. It is hard to lose a mate. It is hard to lose a child. It is...one of the greatest pains one can face."

Ruth nodded.

Mishe paused and said, "There are things I need to tell you...things that I should not discuss now, given all you have shared. You are in pain. I will rest for a while and when I return, we will discuss things. Please...just rest. The poison is a difficult thing for humans to digest. It is better if you give your body time."

"Can it wait?" Ruth asked.

Mishe nodded. "There is still time." She paused as she rose and said, "I am sorry. Please believe that."

CHAPTER SEVEN

RUTH FADED IN AND out of sleep on the couch, her body aching, the room spinning around her when she opened her eyes. She woke to the sound of the dog barking and she saw the Werros coming back down the stairs.

"It is near nightfall," Mishe said. "I must go out soon. We should talk now... It is about what you said earlier. I have thought about this and I believe I know what is happening, albeit, given what you have said to me, this may not be easy for you to hear."

Ruth looked up groggily.

The creature said, "You said you did not know how my kind does these things. It occurs to me that it may be important to tell you now."

"Okay," Ruth said, sitting up. "Hit me."

Mishe sat down. Ruth was unnerved as she moved with more awkwardness, her poise replaced with nervous energy. She could almost pass for human even now.

She explained, "I have told you before that most of my kind are female, yes? Our reproduction is an issue of great concern. My people have faced a crisis for over a hundred years. Before my time, though not much before, we were often conceived and born much as humans are. A male of our species couples with a female to create a child with traits from both parents. It is not known when or why, but about a century and a half ago, our males became sterile."

"All of them, at once?" Ruth asked skeptically.

The Werros shook her head. "We do not know. We are not a fast-breeding people; it was perhaps decades before it was declared that there were no more fertile males. Still, we have survived. Since time was recorded, our females have been able to create children outside of the act of copulation. They are able to conceive a child with male or female partners, so long as they consumes enough of their partners' essence. Each child resembles their mother so nearly that it is almost like she has made herself anew. Some can see the other partner's traits in their features, but the child will be almost twin to her mother."

"What exactly do you mean *essence*?" Ruth questioned.

"That is a very good question, human. We have only lore and experience to teach us. Some learning from your world, when there are those who go live among you for a time. I was taught that females most easily conceive by drinking Werros blood. Among us, this is a most sacred and holy act, to offer one's blood to feed another. It is...a communion, a bonding unlike any other. Sex is a mere act of passion. Consumption is an act of transcendence."

Ruth let out a quiet "Huh."

Mishe laughed. "I reveal to you the divine mystery of my people and that is all you have to say, Ruth?"

Ruth admitted, "It's a lot to take in, Mishe."

Mishe gave a shrug and the gesture was so eerily human that Ruth shivered.

The Werros continued, "This practice, of conception without sex, was not uncommon throughout our history. But when the males became sterile, we were forced to resort to this fully. The problem is, this method only produces females. Which, you see, only makes the issue that much worse. We have so few men left and with them will go our diversity, our...vitality. To see the same faces again and again over the centuries...to have each generation be identical to the last...some say it is the end of us. Those who are unable to accept this have taken to darker ways of reproduction."

Still bewildered, Ruth asked, "What exactly do you mean?"

Mishe hesitated and then explained, "We have known for a very long time that humans are close enough to us, as a species, to act as the second parents. My kind has been drawn to yours for so long. It is understandable. There is no species in this world we are closer to than yours. It is natural that occasionally bonds occur between us. Over thousands and thousands of years of humanity on this continent, there have been Werros with human parents. But this is greatly discouraged, for many reasons. It is simply not practical, either drinking the same human's blood over such a long period of time or to risk being found by killing one and drinking it all at once."

"And what about the other way?" Ruth questioned. "What about sex?"

Mishe sighed. "Our kind are compatible, but humanity is such a diverse and vibrant species, designed to constantly adapt. My understanding is that sexual intercourse could in theory lead to a child, but I have seen no proof of it. But in consumption...there is something in you, some fire that refuses to go out. A child created this way, with a human parent providing its essence, that child is no twin to their mother. Sometimes, they are even born male."

Ruth felt her bile rise and she tried to swallow it down as Mishe continued, "I have heard of kin-circles who are attempting to create male children in order to increase our numbers. They are important in religious ceremonies and they are necessary in order for our way of life to stay the same. A female creating life on her own is difficult at best. We need diversity as much as any other species and our pool is only growing smaller. It would make sense why she—the Werros who attacked you—could not risk drinking from you. She needs as much chance at a male as possible."

"I'm going to be sick," Ruth muttered, putting her head in her hands.

"Listen to me, human," she said quietly. "We will not permit this creature to continue this vile hunt. My people will not allow—"

"You claim a lot of things your people don't do," Ruth accused, glaring up at her, "and yet I keep seeing corpses on my property. And you claim you're going to fix this but all you have done is nearly gotten yourself killed twice and drunk my blood yourself. So excuse me for not being so confident that you're going to fix this."

The Werros said nothing and Ruth stood.

"I think it's best if you leave," Ruth said quietly, swallowing hard. "You can wait until dark, but then I want you gone."

The creature insisted, "What is happening here is rare. I have lived 142 years. I was a child at the same time your country was. I saw humanity through so many wars and plagues. I watched from the forests, only rarely ever venturing out. I have lived 142 years and you are only the second human whose blood I've drunk. So please...un derstand. My kind does not spend our time hunting humans down. We live so apart from you. What is happening...this is something unexpected from all else. I will go if you wish me to, as this is your home. But I think we both want peace. This will only bring my people out of hiding, force them to adjust to human society. And it will be bloody. It will be violent. Your people will probably win in the end, but you will lose so much. And my people... We are dying already, Ruth. I am one of the youngest of us left. Please. Please, I need your help. It is clear to both of us I cannot do this on my own."

"Why me?" Ruth asked.

She said, "Because when you could have killed me, you let me live. You showed mercy. But you were not afraid to take that shot, even when you were dying. Because you do not want another to suffer as your brother did, even though you hated him so."

"How do you know that?"

"I felt it when I first drank from you," she said. "There is already a bond growing between us. You feel it too. I can trust you. You are good."

Ruth swallowed hard and said, "I... I don't know what I can do."

"You can keep me safe during the day," she said, "and you can find out other things, go where I cannot go. I can do the same. I'll even try not to get shot as much."

Her faint smile made Ruth uncomfortable.

"What will you do to her when you find her? That other Werros?" Ruth asked.

"I will kill her," Mishe said simply.

"Even if she's pregnant?" Ruth asked.

She did not hesitate. "Yes." Seeing Ruth's horror, Mishe explained, "I know this seems harsh but what has happened here cannot happen again. The others will know that there is still justice. There must still be order among us, honour."

Ruth asked, "But what if she's carrying a boy, what if—"

She said quietly, "If she is still hunting to this extent and refused your blood, it is likely that she is not carrying your brother's child."

"Small mercies," Ruth sighed, putting her head in her hands again.

Mishe admitted, "I understand the compulsion she has... I sympathize. But it is not the right way. In the old ways, after a child was conceived, the entire kin-circle would feel the pregnancy, would care for the child. Mates came and went, we live for so long, after all. But this way... It is unnatural, and it is wrong. Mates should consent, both of them."

"You said that you and I are growing a bond—"

She shook her head. "No. The one carrying the child... It is difficult for you to comprehend, but suffice it to say there is no accidental pregnancy among my kind. I am not one who takes what is not given. I would not do this to you. The bond is not strong enough, regardless."

"So I've got that going for me at least," Ruth muttered.

"I have confronted her twice in this territory and she has not stirred," Mishe said. "There must be something about this place that draws her. This is a small community; her prey will be noticed. There are denser woods elsewhere. I do not know what could hold her here."

Ruth remembered the claw marks on the ground and she whispered, "David."

Ruth ran out the door, barely getting her boots on before reaching the ground. Mishe followed barefoot as Ruth made it to the grave, kneeling in front of it before pushing the snow away as best she could.

"I saw claw marks in the ice," Ruth explained, trying to reach the earth. "It looked like someone was trying to get in. Was it trying to eat the rest of him or something? Would that have gotten her what she wanted?"

Ruth felt the layer of ice, her hands tracing the marks across it. She shivered as the cold reached her. Mishe stood behind her, watching without answering.

Ruth looked up, her teeth chattering as she waited for the creature to comment.

She said nothing and went back inside.

Ruth stayed for a moment, looking at the headstone. The question formed in her mind, but she could not express it. *Why him? Why start with him?*

She went back into the house, seeing the Werros beside the fire, stoking it back to life.

Mishe said, "Sit down."

Ruth did so, rubbing her arms for warmth as Mishe sat across from her.

She said, "I will need to go to my kin-circle. There is more I need to know that I will not be able to find here. But I do not want to leave you here alone."

"I'll be okay," Ruth said. "She's not interested in me."

"She has her poison in you," Mishe said, touching Ruth's jaw. "I have done what I can...but you know already what the poison is like. You will see things, things you do not wish to see. It may be days before it is out of your system."

"I'll survive," Ruth argued. "This is my home and my property. I'm not leaving it for her. You go and find out what you can. If she comes near me, I'll shoot."

Mishe smiled softly and said, "That seems to work for you."

Ruth hesitated, watching the pulse in Mishe's neck, knowing it was her blood in her veins. Mishe watched with anticipation, tilting her head to look into her eyes. Ruth looked away quickly and said, "You better go."

She nodded. "I can pass for now. I'll be back when I can. If you need of me...well, you will know what to do."

Ruth was puzzled but she did not stop the creature from walking out the door and running into the forest.

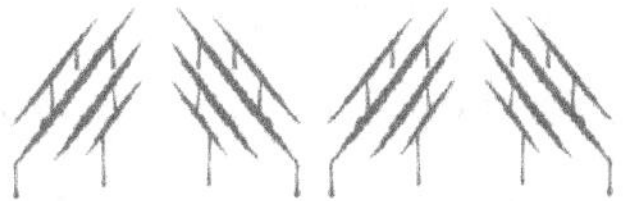

She knew it was a dream. She could feel the fever still, the cramps in her belly, even as the memory played out.

Ellie. There she was. Just a little over two months pregnant. She was just sitting across from her on the deck. She thought she could see the baby bump already, but Ruth couldn't see it. She could just see her. Her lovely dark skin against the blue bikini, her hair freshly washed and smelling so wonderful. Ruth wanted to hold her, wanted to cradle her in her arms and promise her anything. She wanted so badly to touch her.

Ellie again in that purple dress Ruth loved. She was lying on her belly, reading her favourite book and marking the passages she loved best. She was planning to read it to the baby, but was going to be sensible and wait until she could hear.

A girl. Ellie had been insistent that it would be a girl.

Ruth wanted to hold onto that time. She was at Ellie's parents' house. Ellie was the last child of six. Her family was so big and loud and they had embraced Ruth wholly as she was.

Ruth was in the backyard, playing with Ellie's nieces, one of them attempting to tackle her. Ruth let her, the child climbing on her back and shouting, "I am Jack the Giant Slayer!"

Ellie laughed from the side of the porch, her sisters tending to her and chatting about their own pregnancies. She looked at Ruth then with such a smile, a look of utter contentment. It was Ruth's favourite smile. The one she would remember for the rest of her life. Never before and never again would she be so loved.

Ellie in their bed, her eyes closing after sex. Ruth had been so tender with her, so gentle. She only wanted to explore her changing body, to remember this. Ellie had fallen asleep with her makeup on, her mascara smearing against the pillow. She already felt softer to her.

That scene faded as Ellie started crying, crying louder than Ruth had ever heard, crying so hard Ruth thought she might just break in two. She didn't know what to do, what to say. Ellie threw a stuffed animal at her head, wailing.

Keening.

That last time. The desperate lovemaking on the ground as they both cried. In two weeks, it would be over. Everything they had, everything they ever wanted was dead as chaff on the wind. Ruth closed her eyes, trying to remember, trying to remember those last kisses before the end.

She stirred, looking up from the couch to see David at the kitchen table. He drank his coffee without noticing her, without acknowledging that she was there. He was younger then, a little leaner, a cut across his cheek she didn't remember.

She went out to him, reaching to try to touch him, but her fingers felt like they hit a wall of glass. She saw her sisters chasing each other in the living room and she wandered like a ghost, trying to call out to them.

She saw her father sitting in his armchair, watching her over the top of his newspaper. When their eyes met, he unfolded it further and buried himself inside.

She went outside into the summer heat, seeing Mum and Ellie on the porch together, laughing about something. She saw the little girl, running toward her, little pigtails flying behind her as she vaulted into Ruth's arms.

She held her daughter to her chest, smelling her hair. She smelled like Ellie. She smelled like their apartment in Toronto. She smelled like freshly cut grass and sunshine.

Then, back in the present moment that was all too real, Ruth found herself alone and cold on her bathroom floor, shaking as the poison started to fade again from her system. She wanted to call out to Mishe, only to remember that the creature was gone. She stumbled, pulling herself to the bedroom. She collapsed in the bed and dreamt of nothing.

Ruth woke in the night, hearing her cell phone ring beside her. She blearily picked it up, answering, "Hello?"

"It's Naomi."

Ruth sat up, pulling the blankets around her. "Is everything okay?"

"Mum told me what happened. Well. She told me about you throwing her out of the house and threatening to kill her. I'm sure you had good reason though."

"Jesus," Ruth muttered. "How bad is it?"

"Well, she thinks you're going to hell, but that's nothing new," Naomi commented. "She's threatened to make us move back in with her, but that's died down. You're definitely not invited to Christmas though."

Ruth paused. "What day is it today?"

"The eighth," Naomi answered. "Seems weird celebrating this year."

Ruth asked, "You guys going to be okay?"

"Yeah, we'll be fine. I just wanted to let you know that, well, you're a good sister. Esther was telling me about your chat the other day. I don't want to be all mushy but, for what it's worth, you were a better mother than she ever was."

"That's laying it on a little thick."

"I'm being sentimental. Enjoy it while it lasts."

Ruth chuckled. "Okay."

Naomi said, "Hey, I know you're settling things out there and apparently there's a big-ass bear running around. But if you need some company, I can always come out there."

"I appreciate it," Ruth admitted. "I'll let you know."

"Take care of yourself. I'll phone you when the embargo is over."

"Thanks. Love you."

"Love you too."

Ruth hung up the phone and walked out into the hallway. She glanced at the grandfather clock, recognizing it to be just before midnight. She shook her head at her sister's sleep habits and went downstairs.

She plugged her cell phone into the wall, seeing a text message from two days before. She cursed the reception and tapped on it.

It was from Ellie. It said simply: "I hope you're doing okay. I'm thinking of you."

She wanted to laugh, but instead she just deleted it and went back upstairs.

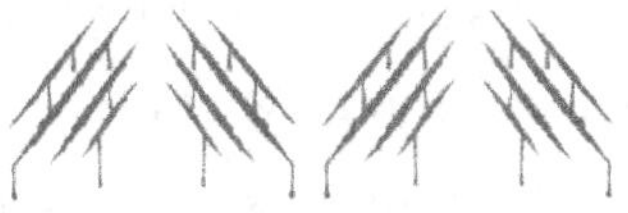

The snow grew thicker. The winds howled as the storm overtook the farm. The landlines were down, and the electricity failed. Ruth could barely make it to the barn and back. She had lit the fire and made a bed on the couch, bringing in the dog as she huddled in blankets for warmth.

She was half asleep, a cup of nearly frozen tea tilting dangerously in her lap when she heard a slam at the back door. She moved the tea to the coffee table, pulled a blanket around her like a cloak and walked into her kitchen. She opened the door, the snow blustering in around the figure standing there.

Mishe.

The creature stood, her hair frozen to her scalp, her pupils fading. She looked up and asked, "Can I come in?"

Ruth nodded, shutting the door behind her.

Mishe stepped forth, walking toward the blanket huddle in the living room. She sat by the fire, wrapping a quilt around herself.

"My kin-circle has moved on," she said quietly. "I must go after them...but I do not wish to leave you here. You will come with me."

Ruth glanced around at the house, hearing the groans of the walls against the wind.

"What did you see this time?" she asked.

"I saw our baby," Ruth said with a half smile. "I saw my dad. I saw Ellie, when we were happy. But I saw a lot of other things too..."

"Some humans think the poison is a blessing, but I think it would be painful when you are so unable to control it."

"Does it affect you?" Ruth asked.

"No, but it does increase the bonding. It is usually done in kin-circles, the act helps cement relationships."

"It's not going to turn me into one of you, is it?"

She smirked, her teeth glinting in the firelight. "I am not a vampire and I am not human. I never was, I never will be. It would be as if an ape bit you. You wouldn't become one of them, would you?"

"Apes do a lot less blood sucking generally."

Mishe said, "I am not injured nor starving. I will be doing significantly less 'blood sucking' myself for a time. Unless…"

Ruth heard the hesitation and replied, "Could you… Could you control what I saw?"

She shook her head. "I can only express happiness, positivity. It is your mind that translates that feeling, especially in these early stages of a bond."

Ruth felt uncomfortable and stood. "When do we go?"

The creature replied, "When the storm ends. The forests are full of your hunters now. It is best I go out the front door with you. I look human enough for now. We will take the back roads if you are willing to drive. You do not run as fast as I do."

"The missing pupils thing gives you away," Ruth commented.

"That cannot be helped right now," she said, looking away.

Ruth shook her head. "It's okay. We're helping each other, right?"

Ruth held out her hand and sat beside her. Mishe kissed the inside of her wrist, kissing up her arm until she found the spot she wanted. She bit down softer than before. The pain was less intense and Ruth lay back, letting the Werros kneel beside her, her lips sucking at the skin.

Ruth felt as if she were spinning, the room growing darker as she grew lightheaded. She wanted to tell her to stop, but the feeling grew softer, more comforting. She felt like she was naked in linen sheets, the sheets soft around her body on a cool summer's morning. She felt her hair long again, flowing around her shoulders as she leaned over to her side. There was a woman in bed beside her and Ruth half expected to see Ellie again.

The woman asleep beside her was familiar, but Ruth could not place her features. The woman stirred at her touch, smiling as she curled into Ruth's frame. Her naked body pressed against her as they kissed. Her hands were in Ruth's hair as Ruth ran her hand down the woman's hip; she groaned Ruth's name in her ear.

Ruth knew the voice. She was vaguely aware of the creature's mouth on her arm, of the cold room around her. She knew the voice of the woman, knew the lips against her skin. She felt a flush of embarrassment, but she gave into the temptation, feeling her body, their lips meeting in a hungry kiss.

The Werros let go of her skin and Ruth startled as she came back. Mishe's eyes met hers, her face gaining its colour, her eyes growing more and more human.

"I wanted you to feel warmer," she said. "I hope I was successful."

The air hung heavy as they looked at one another, each waiting for the other to respond. Ruth's hands cupped Mishe's face before she kissed her. She tasted her own blood, but she didn't care, pushing the creature down into the blankets.

The creature kissed her back, her hands sliding down Ruth's body as they tossed their clothes to the floor. Mishe's mouth settled into her shoulder as she bit down. Ruth groaned, but no visions came. All she felt was then and now, the poison pulsing through her like a drug as the creature drank.

Ruth felt the sensation stop suddenly as the creature pulled away, her body looking even more human, more and more like a flesh-and-blood woman.

"I will not sleep now," she murmured, hesitating before kissing her forehead.

"Good, you can keep me safe," Ruth whispered, sleepily, her eyes closing.

"I'll try my best," she said quietly.

Ruth felt the warm, breathing body beside her, the fire roaring behind them. She gave into the heaviness of her eyes and fell asleep.

CHAPTER EIGHT

R UTH WOKE AS THE overhead light flickered on. The creature stood before her, yawning.

"The storm is fading now," she said. "We should go while there is daylight."

"I guess it's okay to head out," Ruth said, rising.

Mishe yawned once again. "Your human blood is making me sleepy. I'll be watching television while scratching myself by tomorrow."

"Have you seen much television?" Ruth teased, getting up to make coffee.

"A little," the Werros said. "During the 1950s, I spent a time pretending to be a governess. My kin-circle did not approve, but it is not uncommon for our kind to pretend to be human for short periods of time. It was only a few years, but I enjoyed it."

"Why did you leave?"

"Children grow old," she reminded her. "I live much longer than humans do. It would have seemed strange if I remained with them unchanged for so long."

"How old do your kind live to be?"

The creature shrugged. "I honestly do not know. We do not keep the same sorts of records that you do. My kin-sister remembers being in the Haitian revolution. Another claims to remember the first days of the Haudenosaunee Confederacy. We have many old ones among us. I have never seen one of mine die from natural causes such as illness or the like. Many die from being hunted by some rival groups, by humans, by other predators in the forests. I know I am 142. I know I was born in the forests outside Belleville sometime in the spring in the dark, but that is all."

"I guess I must seem like a child to you," Ruth laughed. "I'm only twenty-nine."

"But that is much older for your kind," Mishe said. "It is all relative. Though I suppose I do not know how long I will live. Perhaps 142 is old among my kind."

"Where will your kin-circle be?" Ruth asked.

"Farther north," she replied. "There is a settlement just north of your city Timmins. It is several hours away from here by your vehicle. You will need to dress warmly. I cannot guarantee how well sheltered you will be from the cold."

Ruth said, "I just need to drop the dog off and ask Trip to keep an eye on the animals here. We'll leave right after."

"Is it wise for your family to see me?"

Ruth paused, looking over her briefly. She felt a flush come to her cheeks. While she didn't exactly count what had happened last night as sex, something had shifted. Maybe it was because she looked more and more human, maybe...it didn't matter. She felt different about her now. It only concerned her.

Ruth said finally, "It's okay. You'll stay in the back of the truck. If anyone asks, you're a friend from Toronto just seeing your family up north, okay?"

The creature nodded.

They dressed and went out to the car, Ruth reminding Mishe to keep her coat on. Cora did not stop barking until they finally made it to Trip's place, about ten kilometers away.

She opened the truck door, the dog running out into the snow, happily barking at them. Trip was a tall man, strong from years of hard labour. It was rather amusing to see him bend down to pick the small thing up, rubbing her belly.

"Rue." Trip grinned. "It's good to see you. I heard you've been sick. You want to come in for a little while?"

Ruth apologized. "I can't, sorry. I have to drive a friend up Timmins way. She's had some trouble in the city, needs to go visit her folks."

Trip glanced back, seeing Mishe in the back of the truck. "Sorry to hear that. How long do you think you'll be gone?"

"Just a day or two," Ruth said. "I know, it's shit timing, but I can't leave her stranded here. You'll keep an eye on things for me? There haven't been any bear sightings for a while, but I just want to make sure the animals are okay."

"Of course," he said, nodding. "We'll be fine here. I'll tell the girls. Listen, I heard about what happened with your mom. We both know my sister can be a real piece of work. I'm sorry kid. She'll come around eventually. Just hang in there."

Ruth nodded curtly, walking back to the truck. She waved briefly before starting the engine again.

Mishe mimicked the gesture and Ruth rolled her eyes, putting her arm back down.

They pulled out of the driveway, making their way to the highway. Mishe leaned out the side of the car, blinking as she watched the sun across the snow.

"What do you normally do during the day?" Ruth asked, glancing over.

"We blend into our environments well. We usually don't sleep straight through the night. Ones who drink more human blood sleep closer to a human's sleep schedule. The daylight doesn't blind us as much. How long will it be?"

"Maybe ten hours," Ruth said. "Nine if we're lucky. We'll go up through North Bay. I didn't get to check the roads, but hopefully this storm stayed south."

Ruth glanced over, seeing Mishe's eyes flutter as she tried to stay awake.

"Get some rest," Ruth said. "I know my way north from here. I'll wake you up when we get close."

Mishe nodded, closing her eyes as she drifted off. Her skin paled, shimmering like translucent scales. Her breathing slowed to almost nothing.

Ruth tried not to feel alarmed as she kept driving.

Near dusk, she saw the signs for Timmins. She pulled over at the first gas station she saw, yawning as she pumped fuel into her truck. She reached for her phone, but then remembering some news special Ellie had made her listen to, she left it in her pocket.

She turned, looking at Mishe, who was now stirring. She yawned almost like a cat, shuddering as she stretched, lengthening almost impossibly.

After Ruth paid, she came back to the car, and Mishe indicated the road ahead.

"It's farther north," she said. "There is a lake shaped like the crescent moon. You will see it in time. We are not far now."

It was dark as they pulled to the side of the unplowed road. The creature took off her human clothes, folding them on the seat. Ruth followed her outside, holding her coat close to her.

The Werros hesitated. "I do not know if it is wise for you to follow me."

"You want to leave me here alone to freeze?" Ruth suggested.

Mishe paused and nodded. "Follow then."

They walked into the snow-covered forest, coming toward the edge of the frozen lake. Ruth hesitated as the creature walked forth, her feet light against the ice. Ruth followed, hearing the ice shift underneath her feet, crackling. She kept her eyes forward, watching the creature ahead of her.

They went out about 500 meters until they arrived at a small island in the middle of the lake. Ruth breathed a sigh of relief as her feet once again touched the ground. She heard the Werros stop and she looked up, seeing the six bodies standing before them. Ruth had been growing used to Mishe's more human form and the shock of these strange beings caused her to catch her breath. They were bright and slender, slashes of white like birch trees among evergreens.

Mishe went forward, wordlessly greeting each. As Mishe stepped back, Ruth heard a deep, rumbling laugh that made her feel weak in the knees. She had wandered straight into the lion's den. This is where she would be devoured alive.

The tallest of the six approached Ruth. The creature cupped her chin, pulling her forward to better examine her bruised jawbone. Ruth gazed into its pupil-less eyes, the grey irises focusing on her. The Werros leaned in closer, its inhale sharp against Ruth's cheek. Ruth fought the instinct to run, her body insisting that she was in the presence of a predator she had no chance against. Ruth felt like she was being assessed, like a horse forced to hold still as a buyer decided whether or not it was fit to ride or render.

The Werros pulled away and guided Mishe to the side. It spoke to her in hushed whispers. Their language sounded like no words Ruth had ever heard. It sounded just like breathing. When they finished, Mishe returned to Ruth's side and the elder stood amongst the rest of the kin-circle.

Ruth whispered to her friend, "Who is that?"

Mishe murmured, "My great-grandmother, Obe. Answer whatever she asks of you without any hesitation. She will know if you are lying."

Obe questioned, "You have seen the one we seek?"

Ruth nodded. "Yes, once. She nearly killed me."

Mishe said something quickly, the others looking to each other.

Obe asked, "My kin daughter tells me that this *hea* killed your brother. Tell me, do you grieve his loss or relish in the brutality of his end?"

Ruth replied quietly, "I don't wish a death like that on anyone, not even him."

Obe's expression shifted, but Ruth couldn't read it. "No? You do not believe in justice? In doing what must be done, regardless of how distasteful it might be?"

Ruth said honestly, "I think we're all worth more than the worst thing we've ever done. David hurt me, deeply, and I don't think I'll ever forgive him for it. But I saw what your...*hea* did to him and I don't intend to let that happen to anyone else."

Obe glanced to Mishe. "Your human is a pacifist."

In shock, Ruth laughed. "I don't think I said anything—"

Ruth's throat tightened as Obe stepped close; her words cut off from her. Mishe hung her head, avoiding Ruth's pleading eyes as Obe towered over Ruth. Ruth looked up at her, trying to keep her breathing steady.

Obe said coolly, "You misunderstand me, human. To your kind, there are options other than violence. You attempt to contain problems, to coddle them until they resolve themselves. That is not our way. We do not cage the serpent—we slice its head off."

Ruth managed hoarsely, "Cruel to kill a snake for being a snake."

Mishe said something softly in their language and Obe turned to her. Mishe said something insistently and Obe seemed to relent a little, bending her forehead to press against Mishe's before putting a protective arm around the younger Werros's shoulders.

Obe said, "There is much to be discussed. I have all the answers I need from you, human. There is no need for you to remain here."

Ruth turned to Mishe, "That's it? That's all you needed me for? A ride?"

Mishe opened her mouth to speak, but Obe interrupted. The pair exchanged a glance and Mishe bowed her head in reverence to her.

Obe stared into Ruth's eyes. "I no longer believe that there is anything else you can offer us. Your task is done, human. Leave."

Ruth hesitated and Mishe said softly, "Just go."

Reluctantly, Ruth left, feeling their eyes upon her as she made her way over the ice. A large crack made her jump, but she slowed her heart, walking as softly as she could until she made it back to the shore.

She looked back out over the water and shook her head. She was heading home. If her part in this was over, fine.

Ruth barely made it back to Timmins before she had to pull over. The snow was growing thick and heavy, building faster on her truck than the wipers could push it away. She was tired of driving anyway and her sunglasses were no longer useful against the snow glare.

It was near ten at night now. There weren't many reputable places open this late. Just the bars and the liquor store. After the experience of the last few days, she knew better than to drink alone.

She pulled into the first dive she saw, parking the truck as best she could given the storm. There was a bit of a hotel above the place; she would stay there until daylight.

The manager grinned at her as she stripped off her layers of coats.

"Nice weather, eh?" He chuckled.

"Could be worse," Ruth joked.

She went into the bar, sitting down on a stool with a groan.

"Hey, the kitchen still open?" she asked the bartender.

He shook his head. "Nah, cook couldn't come in with this storm. I've got some peanuts and chips in the back. Will that do?"

She sighed. "It'll do."

He came back with her snacks and she handed him a bill. She ordered a Keith's and looked over at the man beside her, nodding. He was an older fellow, drinking quietly.

"You from out of town too?" he asked kindly. "It seems a few of us got stuck here in the area. I was visiting my sister out in Sioux Lookout. I'm heading back home."

"Where's home?"

"Lindsay."

She chuckled. "You must like your sister; that's a long drive."

He shook his head. "I hate flying, what can I say? Where you headed?"

"I live a bit northeast of Owen Sound."

"I've always liked that area," he said fondly. "I used to go out that way for the summer a lot. We'd do the Elvis festival and then go over and do some fishing out that way. My wife used to like to go up there to see the fish jumping."

"Big Elvis fan?"

"I used to compete," he chuckled. "Won myself second place once. I figured after all those years, it was time to call it quits. Elvis died young; you know, it ruins the illusion when there's an old geezer like me up there."

They drank together for a while. Ruth was on her third when the bar started to fill, younger folks from Timmins, older folks filling the pool tables and bar stools. The college crowd seemed to enjoy rural bars. They joked all the alcohol is the same colour, all poured from a jug marked XXX.

Ruth didn't mind the joke. She had actually been to a bar like that once on the Bruce. It had been a good night, even if she'd had to wrestle a man for a rack of pig ribs. The meat hadn't been worth it, but it made for a pretty decent story.

When Ruth saw her first, she thought the woman must have come in with the student crowd, but she seemed distant from the rest. She stared at her, unblinking as Ruth turned on her stool to face her.

Ruth got up, picking up her bottle as she went into the bathroom. She did her business and washed up, catching a glimpse of her bruised jawline. She touched it gingerly, the skin nearly black when she pressed her fingers further.

She turned, hearing the college students behind her. One asked if she was alright and the other one held out her compact, smiling kindly.

"I've got some concealer too," she offered, "but I don't think it will do much."

Ruth politely refused. "Thank you. I'll be fine. Just smacked myself getting up."

She left, bottle in hand.

The Elvis impersonator was gone from the bar and she didn't feel like going upstairs yet. She wasn't drunk enough. She headed to the edge of the makeshift dance floor, which was just an empty space between tables where the patrons danced.

Maybe it was the storm, maybe it was the dark December night, but there were few happy faces on that floor. She stood at the side, drinking as she watched them dance. There were no cheerful drunks that night.

As Ruth scanned the crowd, she saw her again. She thought the woman had called to her, but as she walked over, she realized the stranger had made no gestures, said nothing. But Ruth felt drawn to her, like a compass turning north.

When she reached her side, they did not touch; the woman made no greeting except her eyes meeting Ruth's. She danced closer to Ruth, staying inches from her even as the floor crowded around them. She looked up with violet eyes, so pale under the harsh light that her irises and pupils seemed to disappear into the whites of her eyes.

She withdrew her gaze from her, and Ruth caught her breath.

"It's you," Ruth murmured.

Mishe beamed, the indents of her teeth against her lips softening as she smiled.

Ruth cupped her face, bringing her mouth to hers, her heart pounding as she kissed her. There were a few hoots, but Ruth ignored them as the creature led them up the stairs, their hands running over each other's bodies.

Ruth felt aflame with each kiss, the liquor pounding through her body. The creature felt so human under her touch, her skin warm and soft, her hair smelling clean and fresh. And her eyes...

They flashed violet as she took off her clothes, the slight fangs glinting as she smiled.

Ruth lost herself, throwing herself at the creature. She had no pride. Not anymore. She had been so alone and now, now she didn't have to be. She didn't have to speak, she didn't have to beg. All she had to do was want and she would receive.

Ruth woke up as the wind howled outside. She stirred, seeing the creature lying in bed beside her, her hair spilled across the sheets, her chest rising with each breath. She woke, turning over to face her.

With newly green eyes, the Werros looked up and down her body with lustful appraisal. Ruth shuddered, seeing how much the creature was growing to resemble her, how more and more human it was becoming.

Ruth rose from the bed, her head pounding as she stumbled into the bathroom. She looked at her own naked form in the mirror, pausing as she saw the faded marks across her legs. The creature had drunk from her again, perhaps multiple times. Maybe that's why she felt so ill.

"So where are we off to now?" Ruth asked as she came back into the room. "Do you need a ride elsewhere? Maybe we can go somewhere even colder, just for fun."

The Werros rose from the bed, grabbing her clothes off the floor.

Ruth paused, watching her change. The dress and leggings the creature wore were definitely not Ruth's. Where had she gotten them?

Mishe said, "My kin-circle wants me to go back to your property. They've informed others in the surrounding areas. She will not be able to escape."

"That quickly? You guys on WhatsApp or something?"

"We have our ways. Are you able to drive in your condition?"

Ruth nodded. "I'm fine. Let's head out."

The creature was oddly quiet as they drove out of Timmins. Ruth occasionally glanced over. As they passed over a bridge, Mishe rolled open her window, breathing in the cold winter air.

Mishe's eyebrows furrowed. "There is something I have not told you yet about my people. Something important."

"Oh? What earth-shattering revelation is this?" Ruth asked.

The Werros said regretfully, "We *lie*."

The creature jumped forth, biting her on the neck and driving something sharp just above her heart. Ruth wheezed as the poison paralyzed her, her throat closing, her hands frozen as the Werros grabbed the steering wheel, pulling it hard to the right. Mishe ripped out what looked like a bone knife and jumped out of the car, rolling off into the snow. The car drove over the barrier, hurling toward the frozen lake.

Ruth wanted to scream as the car broke through the ice, plummeting into the frigid water. She couldn't move as it poured in. She felt her heart race, her body panicking. She willed her fingers to move, but the poison was taking over, slowing down even her breathing.

The poison seeped into her brain and she fell deeper into hallucinations. She was walking back into the coroner's office, her hands shaking. A coroner—not the one she had seen, but a woman—pulled David's body out from its case, uncovering his face.

She could see more than just his torn face. She saw the dip in the sheets where his belly had been ripped from him. She saw the look of fear. She pulled the sheet back farther, seeing his mangled body before the coroner covered him again.

"Is this your brother?" the woman asked softly.

Ruth nodded and whispered with a dark smile, "Yes, that's him."

Ruth came to again as the water filled the car, the vehicle sinking farther and farther into the frozen lake. The cold shocked her, her body unresponsive. The water entered her mouth, trickling down her throat as her heart slowed.

This is it, she thought. *They're not even going to find me.*

She saw Esther running in the field, a ribbon trailing behind her as her pigtails loosened. Naomi ran after her, trying to get her ribbon before it got lost in the grass.

David was just ahead of them, a kind smile on his face. When Ruth's eyes met his, she realized that if she had lived longer, she might have forgiven him after all. But as it was, her heart was slowing to a stop and she hated that her last thought would be of him.

Then suddenly she opened her eyes.

Ruth's heart started again, kicking fast and strong as she looked around in bewilderment. She unbuckled her seatbelt and tried to open the door. When it failed, she punched the unopened window. The glass cracked at her touch and she hit it again, breaking it under her clenched fingers. She pulled herself out, the glass cutting across her chest. She grimaced as she swam upward, her blood trailing down in the frozen water. Her lungs were on fire when she finally reached the surface, breaking through the ice with all of her strength.

She pulled herself onto the surface, coughing up the water in her lungs. Shivering, bleeding, she crawled her way back to the ground, rising weakly, and she threw off her sodden ski jacket, making her way back to the highway.

CHAPTER NINE

SURPRISINGLY, IT DID NOT take her long to be picked up. A stranded motorist freezing to death caught some attention. Her rescuers, an older Ojibway couple on vacation, offered to take her to the hospital, but she asked for the airport. She needed to get home. Now. She couldn't remember why. She couldn't remember much besides the near drowning and the blood pounding in her head. Something was wrong. Something was changing and she needed to lock herself away until she knew what.

Ruth was barely aware as the woman dressed her in her own dry clothes, bundling her up in a worn, soft sweater. Ruth had managed to get out a version of the story: her car had gone off the road and she had nearly drowned.

Her rescuers tried to convince her to go to the hospital, the man especially insisting that Ruth must have picked up an infection breathing in so much water. But Ruth's mind was set. She had to get to the airport and get home. There was something inside of her, something just beneath her ribs that felt utterly wrong. She felt the animal instinct to hide somewhere dark and quiet, a place to either recover or die in peace. She needed to get home.

The couple helped her through security, practically carrying her through the scanner like a bride over the threshold. They would have even walked her on the plane if the stewards let them, but instead the husband left her a Zip-Loc of trail mix and the woman a pair of quarters for the pay phone.

Ruth never learned their names. That would have been the civil thing, getting their number and phoning them later to tell them she got home safe. Maybe she'd even send them a card thanking them, giving them a satisfying end to this interaction instead of just being the strange white woman who had thrown up in their car.

Having paid for her ticket with her miraculously still-working credit card, Ruth shakily made her way to the payphones. She punched in the only number she had memorized in Toronto, sighing in relief when she heard Ellie's voice.

"Babe," she whispered. "I'm flying into Pearson. I'm on the 11 a.m. flight from Timmins. Can you pick me up? I got into this car accident and I'm just so sick and I can't drive home. Please. Baby..."

She realized that she had gotten the answering machine and hung up.

As the plane took off, Ruth stumbled to the washroom, ignoring the flight attendant who politely told her to sit back down. She shakily closed the door behind her, locking it as the woman pounded on it.

Ruth held onto the sink, looking up to see her face. She was sweating profusely, her entire body trembling. She leaned over the toilet, vomiting violently, before she fell to the ground.

The door opened and she looked up blearily, the flight attendant looking more sympathetic this time.

"I'm sorry," Ruth murmured. "I've never been this sick in my life. I didn't want to throw up on the guy beside me."

"I'll get you some Gravol," she said kindly. "I'll help you back to your seat. My name is Amy, by the way. If you need anything, just give me a holler. Poor thing. I had a terrible flu last year. You know you really shouldn't be flying when you're this sick."

Ruth nodded along, letting the much smaller woman help her back to her seat. She buckled back in, shivering under her rescuer's sweater. A moment later, Amy returned, some pills and a glass of water in hand. Ruth took them both without hesitation, her eyes drooping as she tried to rest.

She was in and out of consciousness, only waking fully when the pilot announced they were nearing Toronto. She was still groggy as she stood, her knees weak. She followed the others off the plane, her hand out to steady her.

She arrived in baggage, looking around blearily. She heard Ellie's voice first before she saw her walking toward her. It felt like an eternity for Ruth to take those last three steps to reach her.

"Hey, are you okay?" Ellie asked, just before Ruth stumbled.

Ellie caught her, feeling her forehead. "God, you're burning up, Rue. We should get you to the hospital, I've never seen you—"

Ruth shook her head, murmuring, "Just take me home, baby... Please, I just want to go home."

Ellie kissed her forehead tenderly and put her arm around her shoulder.

"Come on," she said softly. "My car's not far from here."

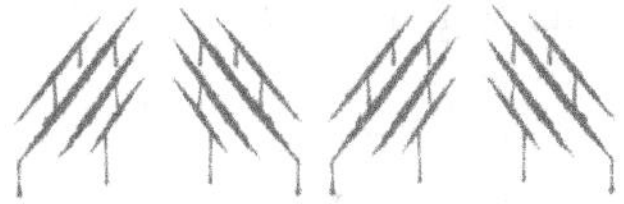

Ruth woke in a cold sweat, gasping as if she had once again been at the bottom of the lake. She looked around, seeing the walls of their once shared bedroom. How? Ruth didn't have her keys...maybe Doris next door had let them in. Ruth looked over, seeing Ellie sleeping beside her in a white undershirt and boxers. Ellie rolled over, stretching as she opened her eyes.

"How are you feeling?" She yawned.

For a moment, Ruth could pretend the last few months had only been a bad dream. She could pretend that they were at home again, that they were together again. That nothing had ever torn them apart.

But she saw the cuts on her hands from tearing her way out of the car, even though they were already fading.

Ellie watched her in apprehension as Ruth stood, still shivering despite the layers that Ellie had dressed her in. Ruth looked out the window, blinking at the sun rising over the cityscape.

"Rue..." Ellie said, rising to go to her side. "Tell me what's wrong. You barely said anything on the phone. Then you show up sick as a dog, no clothes, from a flight from Timmins. Why did you come here?"

"My car was totaled," Ruth said. "I couldn't drive back home. I didn't want to rent a car when I was so sick. I just... I wanted you. I knew you would help me, no matter what."

Ellie put her arms around her and murmured, "You nearly gave me a heart attack at the airport. You looked like you were dying."

I still might be.

Ellie cupped her face in her hands and Ruth pressed her forehead to hers. Whatever urgency she had to get home to the farm faded. She had wanted nothing but this for so long. She wanted Ellie, above anything else in her entire world. Ruth was so weak for her. Ruth wanted to fall at her feet and worship her, plead for her to save her from this raging desire that was suddenly running rampant, this hunger for her.

Ruth kissed her hungrily and Ellie melted into her touch. What followed was quick, almost painful, as their bodies fell back together, as they quenched their thirst for each other. Ruth devoured her, not gaining her fill until Ellie unraveled again and again, until the room smelled only of her once more.

Ruth slept while Ellie read beside her. When she woke, she felt surprisingly well. Whatever illness had taken her seemed to have vanished completely.

Seeing her waking, Ellie put down her book and kissed Ruth's forehead. Ruth looked up at her in adoration, her heart racing at the sight of her.

"I love you," Ruth confessed.

Ellie lay down and nuzzled against her neck. "I love you too, Rue."

Ruth brought her into her arms and Ellie rested against her chest.

"I don't want to be without you, ever," Ruth murmured. "I know... I know I should have tried harder. I should have fought for you. I never wanted to hurt you. I only ever wanted to make you happy. We should have waited until I was done with my dissertation and you had hit five years at the gallery. I felt like I was running out of time to live my life and I wasn't appreciating the life we had already. I... I wanted everything from you and I wouldn't give you anything in return."

Ellie traced her fingers against Ruth's stomach. "You gave me plenty, Rue. I just... I just couldn't live a lie. Not when we were hurting so much. I wanted to scream and you wanted me to just whimper."

Ruth pleaded, "I'll never try to silence you again. I won't hide who you are to me. I'll tell the entire world. Just come back home to me. Please, Ellie. If you want to try again, we can try again, but I just want to be with you."

Ruth brought Ellie's hand to her mouth and kissed it gently.

Silent tears streamed down Ellie's cheeks and she reached up to kiss her. Ruth cradled her in her arms, never wanting to let her go again.

Ellie murmured, "Okay."

Ruth pulled her into a possessive kiss, shielding her face with her hands. Their eyes met and Ruth's body pounded with a sudden need for her. She was hungry for every piece of her. Ellie held onto her tightly, digging her nails into her back as Ruth rolled her beneath her.

Ruth groaned against her skin. "Is this okay too?"

Ellie half laughed and half moaned as Ruth kissed down her belly. "Yes, this is more than okay."

Ruth grinned up at her before she parted her thighs and devoured her.

Ruth woke groggily just before dusk, her head aching as she stood. She blinked, looking into the twilight across the city.

She wandered out, grabbing her freshly washed sweater off the back of a chair. She saw Ellie in the kitchen, humming to herself as she washed dishes. Ruth held her from behind, kissing her neck, freezing when she saw the dark bruise on Ellie's shoulder.

"You were wild last time," Ellie murmured, turning to kiss her. "Whatever's gotten into you, I like it. I like it a lot."

"I... I did this to you?" Ruth asked, trying to hide the fear from her voice.

"Do you not remember?" Ellie asked, frowning. "Are you feeling sick again?"

It all came crashing back to her, the memories she had been keeping at bay. She remembered exactly why she had gone to Timmins. She remembered the creature's bite before she plummeted into the water.

We lie.

In that moment, Ruth was more scared than she had ever been in her life. She was supposed to be dead. She had died. Then she had come back, somehow, become deathly ill, and changed from a gentle service top to a possessive and punishing lover. One who had bitten her love hard enough to leave her black and blue.

If the Werros did lie, what else had they lied about? What had they done to Ruth—what did a bite from a Werros *really* do? What if she hurt Ellie worse? Why had Mishe tried to kill her? And if the Werros thought she was dead, what had happened to the farm? To David's body? To her sisters?

Ruth went back into the bedroom and rustled around her end table until she found her old cellphone, which she had been meaning to recycle for the past three years. She took it in the kitchen and scooped out her water-logged cell from the bag of rice that Ellie had very sweetly dumped it into. She popped out the SIM card and switched it to the old phone. Satisfied that it seemed to pick up a signal, Ruth plugged the old phone into the wall to charge.

Ellie rested against the doorframe, cocking her head as she held her cup of tea.

She asked, "Are you alright?"

Ruth lied, "Fine. I think I just need some air. I'll see you when you're off work?"

Ellie glanced at her phone. "It's only seven, I don't have to—"

Ruth interrupted her with a kiss on the cheek. "I'm going to go for a walk and get breakfast while my phone charges. Maybe hit the gym after. When I'm on the grid again, I'll text you."

Ellie seemed unconvinced, her brow furrowing in an all-too-familiar way. Ruth ignored it, grabbing a jacket and walking out the door. She kept walking, not entirely knowing where she was going. A thousand thoughts were running through her head as she tried to understand what was happening.

She realized her hunger, growling through her entire body. She looked around, noticing a greasy spoon nearby. She stumbled in, ordering the house special, trying to get her head back on straight, trying not to drink four entire Cokes before her food arrived.

The waitress smiled at her as she laid down the steak and eggs, chuckling. "You look like someone who could use a slice of pie for dessert. I'll check what we've got in the kitchen."

Ruth glanced at her nametag—Audrey—nodding as amicably as she could before diving into her food. She devoured everything on her plate, only pausing to drink. Her head started to clear a little once her blood sugar hit acceptable levels.

She was being ridiculous, Ruth thought to herself. She had been sick, sicker than she had been in her life. It could have all been a fever dream, or parts of it. It was hard to keep it all straight in her head.

The snow on top of David's grave, the finger scratches. The woman in bed beside her, not Ellie... Someone with the whitest skin she had ever seen... And the water, the water rushing through the windows.

It couldn't be real. Maybe Ruth had gone on some kind of bender and crashed her own car into the lake. Maybe her rescuers were right, maybe she had ingested something she shouldn't have in the untreated water. That had to be it. She'd rest today and if she still felt like shit, she'd go to the walk-in clinic around the corner.

The waitress returned, concern on her face as she set down the plate.

"We only had cherry left," Audrey apologized. "Ma'am...are you okay?"

Ruth smiled weakly. "Sorry. Just getting over the flu. I'm still a little out of it."

"And the first thing you do is eat everything at this dive?" She chuckled, clearing the empty plates. "Now that's a recipe for disaster. You live nearby? You're okay getting home?"

Ruth nodded, reaching for her wallet, her hand shaking.

She laid some bills on the table before eating the pie slowly, the filling leaking out onto the plate. Ruth paused, looking at the gelled red insides, and felt sick to her stomach. She finished it quickly before throwing her coat back on.

Then she walked out, the door jingling behind her.

She made it only around the corner before she heard the confrontation. Turning toward it, she saw Audrey behind the building, attempting to throw a garbage bag into the dumpster. She was cowering as a man screamed at her, his hand gripping her wrist.

Ruth walked toward them, calling "Is there a problem here, folks?"

The man addressed her. "This doesn't concern you, buddy. My girl and I are just having a little chat. Aren't we, babe?"

Ruth's eyes met Audrey's, waiting for agreement, but the waitress gave the smallest shake of her head and mouthed, *help.*

Ruth got closer and her voice grew firmer. "I think she wants to be let alone."

The man let go of Audrey, snarling as he came to meet Ruth head on.

"I don't think you want to mess with me," he snarled, reaching for a knife.

Ruth reacted, pushing him back against the dumpster and landing a blow to his jaw. She could hear it crack underneath her fist before he threw her to the ground. He jumped at her and she caught him, rolling him over and pinning him to the ground, her hands on his throat before she twisted, his neck snapping beneath her fingers.

She heard Audrey's scream and she blinked, the evidence of what she had done lying still beneath her. She rose, trembling. Audrey stood frozen and staring.

"I didn't mean..." Ruth began, but Audrey ran.

Ruth ran too, stumbling, her bile threatening to rise as she tried to run back home. But a deeper instinct took the place of the nausea, the urge to return to that alley, to tear that body to shreds, to drink his blood drop by drop. She didn't know how, she didn't know why, but one thing was suddenly clear to her.

She was becoming a monster.

Chapter Ten

Ruth wandered the streets long enough to see the sun rise and fall again. She hid in public places, making sure her newly washed face was seen on as many CCTVs as possible. Ruth tried to make it seem natural, that she was shopping for a replacement winter coat and researching possible new cars on a public library computer. Some part of her mind was playing smart, trying to establish an image of a woman who had just gone through a massive ordeal and was far too shaken to have...

Ruth could picture the body every time she closed her eyes and to her horror, she didn't feel regret over his death but at the waste of all that blood.

Ruth made it back to the apartment, sure that she'd have beaten Ellie home by a good hour. Instead, Ellie was already there, waiting at the kitchen table. She was toying with a pencil as if she was working on the *Star*'s crossword, but Ruth knew Ellie only solved puzzles with pens.

With near painful softness, Ellie said, "You never texted."

Ruth confessed, "It wasn't a bear."

Ellie asked, "What do you mean, Rue?"

Ruth whispered, "The thing that killed David. It wasn't a bear."

Ruth tried to say more before she started sobbing, but only got out, "I didn't" before Ellie was holding her and helping her to the couch. Ruth broke down, crying so hard she could barely breathe. Ellie cradled her, murmuring soft assurances as Ruth unraveled and weaved herself together again.

When Ruth could breathe again, she managed, "I didn't kill him."

Ellie assured, "I know, baby, I know. Why don't you tell me what happened?"

Ruth looked up into Ellie's deep brown eyes, filled with such loving compassion that Ruth nearly started weeping again. Ellie still truly loved her.

Ruth sat up, unbuttoning her shirt to reveal the now light-pink line across her chest. Ellie looked startled, reaching out to touch the new scar in wonder.

Ruth explained, "When I got off the plane, this was still bleeding. You know that, you would have seen the gash when you bandaged me and noticed how bloody my clothes were. Ellie, it was deep. I should have gotten stitches. I might have even bled to death. But it's healed. I've been here five days, Ellie. You saw this cut yesterday. Did it look like this?"

Ellie admitted, "No, it didn't."

Ruth sighed in relief, feeling a little less unhinged. "Then maybe you'll believe this part too. There...there's some kind of monster out in the woods, maybe a few of them. One of them killed David and another tried to kill me. The part with the car wreck, that's all true, but there was something in there with me trying to do me in. I think...I think because maybe I'm becoming a monster too."

Ellie considered her response for a moment before saying, "Ruth, I don't know what's going on, but you don't sound like yourself right now."

Ruth agreed anxiously. "I got exposed to their venom and I haven't been acting right ever since. It's been real dark up in my head and this morning—"

Ellie gently pressed her fingers to Ruth's lips. "Baby, you've been really going through it. You're sick, injured, and trying to work through a lot of emotions. Maybe you're just telling yourself a story to make it all make sense. But that kind of coping mechanism isn't healthy in the long run. Do you trust me to find you some help?"

Ruth pleaded, "I know I sound crazy, but it's true, babe, I swear. I get it if you don't believe me, but please, at least trust me."

"I do trust you, but I don't know if you can trust yourself right now."

Ruth could feel the man's pulse beneath her fingers, feel the crack of his spine as she ended his life. No, no, she couldn't trust herself at all.

Ruth said gently, "I need to take care of this, one way or another. Just...I love you. I'm always going to love you. If I never see you again, I want you to know that."

Tears streamed down Ellie's cheeks. "I can't make you stay, Rue. But please. Please, if you love me, stay and we'll get you some help."

Ruth shook her head. "I'd rather believe I was sick. I want to say yes and stay with you until whatever this is either burns out of my system or a doctor figures out how to help me. But if there is even a chance I'm right, I need to find out. I need to make sure that these creatures never hurt any of my family again."

Ellie pulled away and crossed her arms over her chest. She appeared to consider this for a moment and finally asked, "And if it's not true?"

"Then I'll come home to you and get the kind of help you want me to get," Ruth promised. "I love you."

Ellie hugged her tightly and buried her face in her shoulder. Ruth cradled her and kissed the top of her head.

"I wish I could make you stay," Ellie pleaded. "I wish you could just see... Oh Ruth. Oh Ruth, don't make me regret letting you walk out that door. Don't break my heart again. Don't you dare break my heart again."

Ruth tipped up her chin and kissed her just once, soft and sweet, with a finality that was clear to them both. Ruth said nothing else before she took her newly charged phone and dug out her emergency fund hidden under the mattress. Ellie watched wordlessly, silent tears running down her cheeks as Ruth walked out the door.

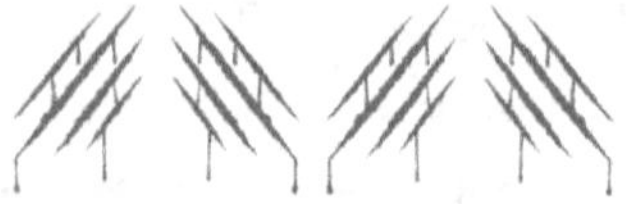

Ruth paid in cash for a terrible car that at least would get her back to the farm. She knew she was headed back to the most obvious place for the Werros to find her, but she had no other choice. She couldn't risk staying in Toronto any longer, not with what had happened, not with Ellie at risk. She didn't know how she would change. She didn't know what she was becoming. She had killed a man. God, she had killed someone. Ruth had always been strong, but never so strong that she didn't know how to wield her strength safely. And the smell of his blood, the taste of it on the air...

Ruth had to find a way to end this. She had to go back to the farm. Maybe Mishe or the rogue Werros would kill her and bury her in the ground beside David.

Or maybe Ruth would get to them first.

Ruth made it back to the house just before noon, surprised to see Trip's car in the driveway. She cursed to herself as she got out of the car.

Naomi came out of the house first, putting her phone back into her pocket.

"What happened to the truck?" she asked.

Ruth looked over at the beater she had bought. "Right. Just trashed the other one. Don't worry about it. I fell asleep at the wheel and hit a tree."

"You were in an accident?" Esther asked fearfully, popping out the door.

"You're all here?" Ruth asked. "Shouldn't you be at school or something? I told you to stay over at Trip's."

"We're picking stuff up like you told us to," Esther said. "What's going on, Ruth? You weren't answering your phone and we didn't know what had happened to you. Where have you been? Were you hurt? Were you in the hospital?"

"I'm fine," Ruth assured them, "but you all need to go back to Trip's. Is he here?"

Naomi shook her head. "He just let me borrow the car. Cora's here though. Come here, girl, you want to see Rue?"

The little poodle waited at the door, baring her teeth.

"Maybe she's mad you left her for so long," Esther quipped. "Come here, girl, it's time for us to go home anyway, let's go."

Cora refused to move, snarling.

"I stayed at a friend's place in Toronto; they had a cat," Ruth lied. "It's nothing. You guys need to get out of here, okay?"

"That's it?" Naomi laughed. "You've just come back and you're kicking us out?"

"Get the hell out of here," Ruth ordered. "I don't want to see either of you here. Is that clear? If you need anything, I'll drop it off myself."

"Jesus," Naomi grumbled. "The police said the bear was found. It's over, Ruth. Can we just come home now?"

Esther said nothing, carrying her bags to the car.

"I'll call you later," Ruth promised. "I'm just trying to keep you safe."

Naomi rolled her eyes, picking up the dog and carrying her into the car. Ruth picked up the rest of their gear by herself and packed them into the car. She was shaking by then, her body growing hot and the sudden hunger in her belly demanding her attention. She waved as they drove off, but the moment they were out of sight she dropped the pretense of humanity and stumbled into the house, locking the door behind her. She barely kicked off her shoes before she made it into the kitchen, pulling out three frozen pork chops and eating them on the spot, her teeth cutting through them like they were just slightly stale bread.

She stood, the melting ice and blood running down her chin. She reached up and felt her teeth. Her incisors had grown more pointed, sharper. She went into the bathroom, washing up. She stood at the mirror, looking over her face. She looked human. Her skin was no paler, her pupils remained present. The teeth were unusual, but they looked close enough to normal that she could probably get away with them. She took off her clothes, which were completely soaked with sweat, and examined the rest of her body. Her legs had grown thick and muscled, unlike how the Werros had looked, but definitely much stronger than she had been a week ago. Her back in particular showed defined, thick muscles running across it and through to her arms.

She also noticed that despite the fact that her bathroom was only five degrees, she was perfectly comfortable standing in her underwear. She was running a lot warmer than she had before. She felt like she could touch the snow and it would melt under her fingers, sizzling.

She should have been afraid of the change. Ruth had spent so much of her life afraid of another raised voice, of another blow. But she felt strong. She felt powerful. And that was what scared the hell out of her. She was adapting far too quickly; it felt too natural to her, the violence growing inside of her. It almost felt... It almost felt like she was not so much *becoming* but *uncovering* what had lain beneath her this whole time.

The thought hit her hard and she crumpled, pulling herself toward the toilet. She vomited until she was empty and passed out on the floor.

There was a hard knock at the door. Ruth forced herself off the floor and back into her clothes. She nearly tripped down the stairs and didn't quite recover by the time she finally answered the insistent pounding. Ruth knew her shock was written across her face and she was too stunned to do anything but stutter out, "Mum? What are you doing here?"

Her mother stood by the door, shuffling her feet.

She said quietly, "I heard you were in an accident."

It took Ruth a second to process what she had said. "Yeah, I'm fine. I just got the wind knocked out of me; that's all."

Mum hugged her tightly, Ruth stepping backward in confusion.

"Oh, my baby," Mum whispered. "I'm such an idiot."

Ruth let herself be held and she kissed the top of her mother's head.

She pulled away, saying softly, "Really, I'm fine."

"We shouldn't fight like that," Mum said. "Especially over the holidays. It's Christmas. You should come over for dinner. Really. I'm so sorry—what I said to you. Just with David, it's all been—"

"I know," Ruth said quietly, not wanting to start a fight. "It's okay."

"You come over for dinner at six, okay? It's Christmas Eve tomorrow. We'll do the big dinner the next day. White Elephant, twenty bucks."

Ruth nodded, in utter shock as her mother waved and let herself out. It had not taken her long to do the math. It had been five days longer than she thought since she left Toronto. Had she lain there, unconscious, for that long?

Ruth found her phone on the bathroom counter. The battery was nearly dead and there were half a dozen texts from Ellie and three times that from her sisters. She looked around for a charger while she scanned through the messages. None of the ones from the girls were urgent but Ruth felt guilty for not being there for them when they needed her.

Ellie's first five were relatively standard, asking if she was feeling better, asking her to phone her when Ruth had a chance, and growing more and more concerned that Ruth wasn't answering her.

Ellie's final text, sent mere hours before, simply asked, *Please still be alive.*

Ruth answered, *I'm safe. I love you.*

Ruth hesitated and then wrote, *Merry Christmas, Ellie.*

She turned off her phone and plugged it into the charger.

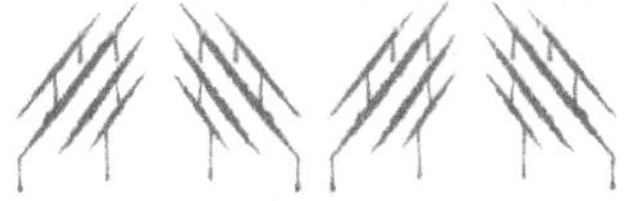

The door to her mother's house opened and Ruth smiled as Naomi greeted her, dressed in a shiny silver outfit that their mother normally would never have let her get away with. It immediately confirmed Ruth's suspicions. Mum was drinking again.

Ruth took off her boots, making her way up to the second floor. A split-level house never left much room in the entryway. She couldn't exactly linger. She had little time to wander anyway before Trip tapped her on the shoulder.

"Can we go chat?" he asked nervously.

Ruth grabbed two bottles of beer from the fridge and followed Trip down the stairs and into the family room where several of her young cousins were playing video games.

He grumbled, finally finding a bean bag chair and pulling it toward the sliding glass door. He offered it to Ruth, who politely refused and sat on the ground beside him. He struggled getting into the chair and settled.

"I know you came back and all for the funeral," he asked, "but what are you going to do with the place come spring? I love the girls, but they can't stay with me. And you know they sure as hell shouldn't stay here. But you want to stay out there? What you going to do a year from now? Naomi might be off at college, but Esther will still be at home. You've never been much for the farm; you couldn't wait to get off it."

"What do you suggest?" Ruth asked.

"Well," he said, "I want to buy it from you. Nah, I know you'd just give it to me, but there's money in that land. You can stay in the house. I just want the property. Stay there as long as you want. It's good for these things to stay in the family. Especially if David's resting there now."

Ruth didn't know what to say. A month ago, this would have sounded like the perfect solution. Now it sounded like a nightmare. The Werros was still out there. She couldn't let Trip take things over when there were creatures out there that might kill him. And she... Well, she didn't know what she was. She had only been awake for a day and nothing had become any clearer to her except that she was constantly hungry and would never need a winter coat ever again.

Ruth admitted, "I'm not sure, Trip."

He said, "Think it over. Stay even until the summer. The girls wouldn't mind living in the city, if you can convince your mother. You know this good cheer is going to stop the minute she needs another bottle. You ain't ever going to have a moment's peace here. You're going to be fighting an uphill battle. It's only fair if you want to bow out now. You're a good kid. You've done your piece."

Ruth said softly, "I can't leave. Not yet."

Trip nodded. "Eh, I imagined that would be the case. It's hard to leave the ghosts behind, isn't it, even when you know you should."

Ruth said nothing and he struggled getting out of the chair.

"Hell of a thing," he said, taking a drink. "This family gets stranger every day."

The children cheered over on the couch as one of them sniped a villain. Ruth stayed on the floor, drinking as she looked out into the thick snow pressed heavy against the glass.

She looked up as Naomi came in, sitting down beside her.

"Can I have a sip?" she asked.

Ruth passed her the bottle. "It's pretty much water anyway."

Naomi drank without flinching. She had definitely had more than a sip before.

Ruth smiled. "What's going on, kid?"

"So are we moving to Toronto with you?" Naomi asked. "Because I don't know how much longer I can stick around here. It's depressing at Mum's and Trip's house smells like stinky, awful boys. And the food's terrible, either way."

Ruth took the beer back. "I don't know. Would you even want to go? You're graduating in half a year. You don't want to spend that time with your friends?"

"I'd do a victory lap, obviously," Naomi said. "Everyone does it now. Then I'll finally be able to take something interesting like... Well, not Welding 301 or something."

Ruth laughed, "Maybe you'd be a good welder."

Naomi said, "I can barely paint my nails straight. I don't think the world is ready for me to enter the trades."

"You tell me something," Ruth said. "How long has Mum been drinking this time?"

"Since you went up north," Naomi admitted. "Ellie called Trip when she was waiting in the airport for you. I shouldn't have said anything about the accident to Mum, but she wondered where you were and—"

"It's not your fault," Ruth reminded her. "She fell off the wagon, you didn't push her."

"Well, it's good to see someone thinks that," Naomi said, rolling her eyes. "Esther's been driving me nuts. She keeps saying we need to decrease Mum's stress and the problem will go away. She's just a drunk, just like Dad. Mum, I mean, not Esther."

Naomi took another swig before handing the bottle back to Ruth.

"Mum talks a lot when she drinks," Naomi said.

"Let me figure this out," Ruth assured her, ignoring Naomi's last statement. "I'll try to figure something out."

Naomi shrugged. "We'll survive. We always do."

They stopped talking when they heard the glass smash upstairs. Ruth and Naomi walked up, hearing the argument from the stairs. Ruth saw Esther in the kitchen, crying, her mother yelling at her.

"You said you would pull the turkey out," Mum barked. "Now it's ruined. How are we supposed to feed twenty people? Maybe we should just order pizza, wouldn't that be great?"

Ruth stepped in front of Esther instinctively.

Mum laughed. "Of course. Of course! I am this big evil woman and you have to step in to play hero and save your innocent little sister from me. All I wanted was for her to take care of one thing. I'm busy running dinner here. I think she can handle a little responsibility. She certainly didn't learn that from you."

Ruth felt the anger rush through her, as strong as it was behind the diner. Her hands trembled and she felt adrenaline pump through her heart. She looked over, seeing Naomi standing nearby. Naomi was watching her carefully, waiting to see how she would react. Ruth forced herself to stay calm, focusing on her breathing, even though every fiber of her being wanted to deck her mother out cold.

This isn't you, Ruth thought to herself. *This is the poison.*

The rage in her fought back until Ruth locked eyes with Naomi. The wild animal in her settled, agreeing silently that it would hold back for her.

Ruth said finally, "Esther, why don't you go get cleaned up? I'll see what I can do to help Mum out."

Mum smirked to herself, walking back out of the kitchen. Ruth examined the turkey, which looked fine to her. She swept up the broken glass, listening to the others continue their mingling. She tied the shards up in a garbage bag and went into the garage.

She turned on the light, startled when she saw Esther sitting on stored patio furniture, smoking a cigarette.

Ruth raised an eyebrow as Esther put the cigarette out hastily.

"I see Mum hasn't gained a sense of smell since I was a teen," Ruth commented. "Come on. I've got some gum in the car. You want to go for a little ride?"

Esther nodded. "I need to get out of here."

"Grab your coat. We've got twenty minutes. Let's make it a country block."

Esther followed her out into the winter, sitting down beside her in the cold car. Ruth started the engine as Esther blew into her hands and rubbed them.

They pulled out onto the laneway, driving slowly down the country road, the snow falling quietly around them.

They were quiet for a few moments until Esther pointed to a field.

"Pull over there," she said.

Ruth did so, letting her sister out. Esther stood in the ditch at the side of the field, looking out onto the snow. Ruth followed, leaning against the car as she gave her sister some space.

Ruth heard her sister crying and came to her side. Esther turned to face her, wiping away her tears.

"I want you to tell me something honestly," Esther asked, looking up at her angrily. "Why do you hate him so much? Why did you hate David?"

"David?" Ruth asked. "I've never said—"

"You hate him," Esther accused. "Did you always? For the longest time, I thought it was me. I thought you stopped caring about us. But it had to be him, wasn't it? The minute he's dead, you have no problem dropping everything to come back. But when he was alive, you couldn't come back for anything. You missed birthdays, you missed when I graduated from Grade Eight, you missed everything! So what did he do? What was so awful that you couldn't even be there for us?"

Ruth felt her heart sink into her chest as she lied, "I didn't—"

"Please," Esther begged. "Just tell me."

"He loved you both," Ruth said, her heart racing. "You need to know that. He would have given anything for the two of you."

"Oh God," Esther whispered. "What did he do?"

"You have to understand," Ruth explained. "He was fifteen when Dad died. We had no idea what we were doing. No one taught us how to be parents, how to suddenly become adults, how to...how to go through what we were going through together. He was trying his hardest."

"Just tell me," Esther insisted. "I need to know."

"Baby," Ruth said softly, pulling Esther toward her. "David loved you and you love him. I love him too. I do. That never changes. It doesn't matter. We fought. We argued. But we loved each other—"

"No," Esther refused, pushing her away. "No more bullshit. This entire family is built on bullshit. I don't want to become you, Ruth. I don't want to take care of her until I just... I want to be happy. Now. I don't want to just keep it all in until I run away. I need to know. No more secrets."

"Okay," Ruth said, making up her mind and clearing her throat. "Here's the truth. When I was in high school, I played rugby for about two years. It was really the only thing I had that was just me, just mine. I had school and I had you two. David...he thought I was being selfish. He thought I should just be at home. We argued and it wasn't a huge deal. But... I met someone. She was... Well, if I'm built like a linebacker, she was built like a tank. But she had the sweetest smile, even when tackling someone. And...we fell in love. She was my first love, my first kiss, my first...other things I'm not talking to my baby sister about."

"Did you know you were gay before that?" Esther asked.

Ruth shrugged. "To be honest, it wasn't something I really thought about much. I just thought I was a late bloomer or something. It never was about the label for me. It makes me feel...itchy. I was just someone who fell in love with a girl. I call myself queer if I need to call myself something. But...anyways. I wanted to tell David. I was in love. It wasn't about coming out, it was about being with her. Her parents were cool with me moving into town with them. We could be together, I could be more serious about sports, about school. I thought I had a chance to be something other than just your big sister."

"What did he say?" Esther asked.

No more secrets. Ruth wanted to honour that, but in the end, she couldn't. The full truth would shatter her. A half-truth was as much as Ruth could give.

Ruth said, "We fought. We argued. He told me I was being selfish and I thought he was being a homophobic prick. We fought until I finished Grade Thirteen. It made it difficult to come home since I knew he didn't agree with me."

"We find strange reasons not to talk to people," Esther said quietly. "I mean...that must have been rough, but, I mean, that was years ago."

"Yeah, yeah it was," Ruth conceded, "but there you have it. Big family secret out in the open."

Esther took a deep, shaky breath. "Thank you for telling me."

"You're welcome," Ruth replied guiltily.

"Come on," Esther said with a smile, "let's get back home. It's time for dinner. Let's give this family togetherness another shot."

Ruth gasped, crawling to the bathroom as her limbs seized on her. She tried not to scream, pulling her way up to the toilet and vomiting profusely. She shook, crying, both cold and hot.

Ellie stood in the doorway, worried and pacing.

"I'll be fine," Ruth said hoarsely, scrambling to grab her bottle of pills. "I just have to make it forty minutes. Go lie down. I'll be there soon."

Ellie took the bottle of pills and poured her a glass of water. She sat on the floor beside her, holding the medication out to her.

"Drink it slowly," she advised. "You don't want it just coming back up again."

Ruth did so, gaining control of her breathing. Ellie helped her to her feet, half carrying her back into the bed.

Ruth lay on top of the covers, still sweating.

"What happened?" Ellie asked, softly stroking her arms.

"Esther asked me the same question," Ruth choked out a laugh. "That's the problem. Everyone wants to know things they don't want to know."

"She asked about David?" Ellie asked.

Ruth nodded.

"What did you tell her?"

Ruth whimpered, "Some sort of version of the truth. What was I going to say to her, Ellie? My little girl adores him. It would just shatter her."

"She was five years old," Ellie reminded. "She might know already."

Ruth shook her head. "I feel like she would have remembered me being in the hospital for eight days." Ruth whispered, "My brother beat the living shit out of me. He beat me into a pulp. He had been beating me for years. It was the only reason I joined rugby in the first place. It was a damn good excuse for bruising. What do I tell her? That he nearly killed me? Better to think he was just your garden variety homophobe instead of—"

"What?" Ellie asked.

Ruth hesitated and finished, "A sick, sick man. Dad beat the tar out of him too. He was a kid and suddenly he had to be a father. He had no other example, no other way. He needed to keep order, control. Part of that was controlling. I wasn't his child, I wasn't his wife. I was...his sister. His partner. And he didn't know how to handle the fact that I loved someone else more. There always would have been something. But that was the thing that nearly killed me. I could have loved anyone and he would have tried to take them from me. I think about it still. I think about..."

She realized Ellie was crying and she held her tightly.

"I'm sorry," Ellie whispered, "I'm supposed to be comforting you."

Ruth murmured, kissing her forehead, "You are. It's hard to pretend. Sometimes it's just...sometimes you just need someone else to hear, to know. It's over. And most of the time, I'm okay. God, I haven't had a panic attack since we lost the baby. Before that, I made it almost two years. I'm okay. I really am. It's just... I feel guilty about how relieved I am that that man is dead. I could have wept for joy. But he was still my brother. I still love him. Worse, I know he loved me."

Ellie said gently, "It's over."

"And if I tell them," Ruth said, "it'll never be over."

Ruth looked up and realized Ellie wasn't there. She shivered more, feeling the poison still in her blood. The monsters out in the forest scared her less, even the ghost of David scared her less than what was growing inside of her. There was something very wrong in her body, something that was changing it cell by cell.

Ruth slept. For how long, she didn't know. She just crawled into bed and didn't leave. The dreams haunted her. She took her drugs when she could and she slept when they would let her.

She was not sure what made her finally get out of bed. She wasn't hungry. She wasn't even thirsty. But her legs had a will of their own, her heart pushing her forward.

Still dressed in her boxers and undershirt, she went down to the kitchen, the sun just beginning to set. She opened the door, the winter breeze cool against her skin, but not unpleasant. She stepped tentatively out, her feet bare against the snow. She grimaced, but she could still feel her skin. She walked out farther, tying her messy hair back behind her. She walked to David's grave, brushing snow off the stone before turning back to the open fields.

Her heart raced, the muscles in her legs pulsing, her body breathing faster. She thought she might be having another panic attack, but this was a different impulse, something primal and utterly necessary.

She ran.

Her feet barely dented the snow as she ran, the wind cold but bearable against her skin. She started panting, her lungs protesting in the snow. When she reached the mended part of the fence, she stopped. No. Not yet.

She looked back at the house and hunger gripped her suddenly. She needed to eat and she needed to eat now.

Ruth ran back to the house, finally out of breath when she made it through the door. The cold finally hit her and she stumbled around until she found her winter jacket to wrap herself in. She went to the fridge and threw some of the leftovers from Christmas in the microwave. She waited impatiently for them to heat up, finding some discarded pants in the meantime.

She tore her food from the microwave, even though the bowl was far too hot. She devoured it with her fingers, but found it lacking. She hunted through the rest of the fridge, discarding almost everything until she found a pork chop she had been defrosting. She ripped through the packaging and ate it raw, groaning as it went down her throat.

Realizing what she had done, she ran to the washroom and vomited in the toilet. She wiped her face and looked in the mirror.

She could swear her fair skin was lighter, her freckles fading. She bared her teeth and she saw the jaw of a predator. She was close. The transformation was almost over. Then she would understand better. Then she would know what to do next.

That night she dreamt of the forests, of David calling out to her while she ran from him. But it wasn't far enough. She screamed out, her nails clawing through the ice as she was dragged into his grave with him.

Chapter Eleven

R UTH WAS PUTTING ON the coffee when she felt her phone buzzing in her pocket. She picked it up, resting it in the crook of her neck as she worked.

"Hey Trip," she answered. "What's going on?"

"Can you do me a favour and pick the girls up today? Naomi reminded me this morning that she's done with her exams at like one or something and refuses to wait for the bus. Well, see, she's got this doctor's appointment, it's all womanly stuff and Susan's busy and well... I think she wants her sister there."

Ruth sighed. "She's not pregnant, is she?"

Trip laughed nervously. "She seemed pretty relaxed about it. Maybe she just wants me off her case, I don't know. I can't keep them here much longer, kid. And if you're sticking around after all, please just take them home."

Ruth said, "I'll pick her up. Esther's okay with the regular time?"

"She damn better be. She's got an exam at 2:30. She ain't missing it."

"Okay," Ruth said. "I can do that."

After breakfast, she headed out of town, north up the Peninsula. She drove through back roads until she found herself alone in the snow-covered forests, without another human in sight. She pulled over and stripped down to her sports bra and shorts, her feet bare as they touched the snow.

She winced at first, but her body adjusted by the time she put her hand against the ground. Her feet grew lighter, hardly marking the snow. She stretched out her arms and legs, tenderly, letting her body adjust to the cold.

And then she ran.

She knew this area well now. She knew the roots of the trees, she knew the creatures that lay within it. She resisted the urge to hunt, reminding herself of the several pounds of beef jerky in the back of the car.

She ran until the thirst faded, until her heart beat loud enough to convince her that she was still human.

She stopped by a river, leaning over as she caught her breath. She could see the steam rising from her body. She raised her hands, watching in curiosity. She paused, her heart skipping a beat.

The freckles had disappeared entirely from her arms this time.

She suddenly felt a chill and she shuddered, holding her arms against her chest. This would have to be enough for now. Exercise seemed to help the rage swings but the longer she stayed out, the more...the more she felt like something else entirely.

Ruth heard sirens as she neared the school. It wasn't unusual since the high school was just across from the hospital, but the three fire trucks that passed her made her worry.

She made it to the edge of the parking lot when she saw the smoke rising from the building. Police were trying to direct cars away from the area; nervous students stood outside on the football field, some cheering, some filming the event on their phones.

Ruth made it to the police barricade, resisting only slightly as someone pushed her back. She looked around at the other parents. Some students who were trying to get into the building.

"Have they evacuated?" Ruth called out to a larger woman ahead.

"Most of them," she shouted back. "They say the top north corner has been blocked off. They're trying to get through, but the ceiling's collapsing everywhere, it's too dangerous."

"Ladies," a police officer ordered. "You have to stay back and let them do their jobs. There's no need to panic."

"That's easy for you to say," a man snarled back. "It's not your kid up there!"

Ruth's heart sank, checking on her phone. Naomi would text. She would call. She loved this nonsense, she would have been talking about it to everyone online.

Unless her phone was still turned off for her exam.

Ruth's hand went to the back of her head, tugging on her hair as she tried to think. She glanced around, seeing the back of the school. She ran.

She heard a police officer yell after her, but Ruth couldn't be caught. She ran toward the back doors, leading into the cafeteria. She threw herself into them, falling to the ground as they gave way, apparently unbolted. She held her arm in front of her face, shielding herself from the smoke. She coughed, pushing forward as she felt her way to the stairwell. She opened the door, the backdraft throwing her on her back. She stood, running through the flames.

She felt the heat, but it didn't sting. She was hotter than the fire. It could not hurt her, for she was made of the same thing.

She pushed up, her lungs crying from the smoke. She ran forward, seeing the crashed beams and rubble across the floor. She dug as quickly as she could, pulling the rubbish away until she heard a teenager's voice crying out for help.

Ruth reached his side. He couldn't have been more than fourteen. She saw his broken leg and moved the tiles off him, tying the wound together with his scarf.

She gently picked him up, carrying him over her shoulder. He whimpered as she went forward, seeing the two classrooms at the end of the hall. One door remained wide open and a brief glance inside showed that no one was there. She felt resistance against the next door and using her free shoulder, she broke it down.

She heard a few screams and saw five teenage girls and one frightened teacher get up from the other side of the room.

"Come on," Ruth called out. "The way's clear, you're going to have to go straight out. Is there anyone else here?"

"Naomi MacGowan!" the teacher shouted. "She was heading back down, she just finished. You didn't see anyone else?"

"Is there another stairwell?" Ruth yelled.

"To the right," she said, "but I don't know if—"

"Get out," Ruth said, handing the boy over to her. "It's clear, but there's a lot of smoke. Go. Now."

She saw the wreckage at the end of the hall, the ceiling collapsing further as the fire grew. She pushed through, breaking down the next door, the clothing burning off her arms. She coughed, making it halfway down the stairs before she saw her sister, pinned beneath a structural beam.

"Naomi!" Ruth screamed.

Naomi looked up at her blearily and started crying, the small shattering cry of a baby pleading without words. Ruth ran to her side, throwing off the beam with ease. She picked her sister up and, seeing the collapsed end of the stairwell, carried her back up and out the way she came. Naomi held onto her, her arms weak around Ruth's neck as she tried to hold on.

Another blast caught them, forcing Ruth to cradle her sister before pushing them out the final doors and onto the ground. They rolled against the concrete, two paramedics rushing up to bring them back toward the others.

Ruth felt a blanket being brought across her shoulders. She looked around for Naomi, seeing her on a stretcher, reaching to grab her phone. Ruth laughed weakly, until she felt her phone buzz in her pocket.

There was a single text from Naomi: *Oh big sister, what nice teeth you have.*

Ruth drove Esther to the hospital, her young sister oddly quiet as Ruth tried to keep herself together.

As they pulled into the parking lot, Esther looked at her curiously and asked, "Are you getting white hair already?"

Ruth glanced at her reflection in the rearview mirror, seeing the white wisps on her left side. Three white stripes snaked through her red hair. It was not like the salt and pepper streaks of age, but like a tree scarred from lightning.

Ruth parked the car and walked into the main entrance, holding her sister's hand protectively. She knew the ER would be chaos right then; there were at least a dozen people with smoke inhalation, more for other serious injuries. The hospital had curtained off a section of the waiting area for families. Esther roamed the gift shop absentmindedly for a while, coming back with a chocolate bar for them both.

They ate quietly, glancing up when a volunteer came up to them.

"Ruth MacGowan?" she asked, smiling kindly. "Your sister is upstairs now if you'd like to see her. The doctor would like to talk to you, too."

The volunteer, an older woman with a slight limp, led them to the elevator, chuckling. "I'm glad I guessed right. She told me a redhead with a blonde teenage girl. I could have been there for a while."

Ruth smiled politely, following her into the children's ward. They entered the ward, going to the fourth bed, near the window. Naomi lay still, her eyes closed, an IV hooked into her arm, and a tube around her nose.

Naomi opened her eyes, grinned, and whispered hoarsely, "At least I finished the exam."

Esther hugged her sister, gently, cautious of the bandaging around her chest.

"I'm fine," Naomi said. "Just some bruised ribs and a broken wrist. They're just keeping me overnight because of the smoke. I'll be out tomorrow."

"Sure you didn't break the wrist on purpose?" Ruth teased weakly.

Naomi met her eyes, shaking her head with a small smile.

Esther sat beside her and the two started chatting. Ruth went out into the hallway, looking for a nurse. She felt a hand on her shoulder and she jumped, recognizing the boy she pulled from the wreckage, limping on crutches.

"Thank you," he murmured.

She nodded curtly and kept walking, seeing a woman wearing a lab coat at the end of the hallway.

"Ruth?" the woman called. "I'm Dr. Kaling. Can we go chat for a minute in my office?"

Ruth nodded, following the doctor into a small office off the corridor. Dr. Kaling closed the door quietly and sat down at her desk.

"Ms. MacGowan," the doctor said. "The police are putting together a report about the incident. I am told that you went into the building of your own volition, rescued eight people including your sister, and that you escaped unharmed. Is this correct?"

Ruth replied, "I'm a little sore and I've got a cough."

"Do you have any training as a firefighter?"

"I'm a librarian," Ruth said sheepishly

"So this was all some sort of adrenaline rush?"

"What is this about?" Ruth asked nervously.

"Frankly," Dr. Kaling said, "they were worried about your mental health. I'm told you recently lost another sibling. A Constable Henley advised us that it might be wise to keep you under supervision, to ensure that another...attempt—"

"I wasn't thinking," Ruth cut her off. "I knew my sister was up there; I needed to help her. He's right. I lost one of them, I'm not losing another."

"Adrenaline can only explain so much to them," Dr. Kaling replied skeptically. "I believe you, Ruth, I do. I've seen reports of mothers lifting cars to save their children. I just have to tell the police that I talked to you and I am confident in your mental state. Which I am. It is miraculous that you were unharmed, but I am not one to toss away a miracle."

Ruth nodded.

Dr. Kaling stood up and offered her hand. "Thank you. You saved a lot of lives today. Just...try not to run into any burning buildings again."

Ruth laughed in relief. "That's the plan."

Dr. Kaling hesitated as she opened the door. "If you need someone to talk to, we have many fine counselors here. Grief is a difficult process."

"I'm okay," Ruth said. "Thank you."

She went back to Naomi's room, standing outside the door as she saw her mother hovering over Esther, talking to her younger daughters.

She could see her mother startle and heard her say, "We'll talk about this when you get home tomorrow."

Mum left in a huff, pausing when she got to Ruth.

"We're having a family meeting tomorrow," Mum said. "We've got to sort out this housing situation. She can't stay with Trip; there's no one to watch her during the day."

"She's almost eighteen," Ruth said. "She'll be fine on her own."

"She could have died today," Mum argued, her eyes red as she looked up at Ruth. "God, if you hadn't been there... I nearly lost both of you. Don't do this to me. I can't go through this again. Please just—"

Her mother fell into her arms and Ruth held her softly, resting her chin on the top of her head.

"It's going to be okay," Ruth assured her. "I promise."

"David used to promise me that," she said quietly. "He used to promise me he'd take care of everything, I never had to worry about a thing."

Ruth said nothing as her mother left her side.

"I'll drive Esther home," Ruth said. "Go sit with Naomi. Let me know when we're meeting tomorrow."

Mum looked at her and touched her face.

"You're bleeding," she murmured. "Go get that looked at."

Ruth sat awkwardly on her mother's couch. She had left her toque on, conscious of the growing white in her hair. She checked her reflection incessantly, worried that her pupils would begin to fade as well.

Ruth sat across from Naomi, her sister's eyes never leaving hers as Naomi said, "I want to live with Ruth."

Ruth argued, "I'm not living on the farm forever. I've got to go back to my thesis in two months and there aren't going to be any jobs up here for me. I know you'd love to move to Toronto, but you've only got a few months left until you graduate; you shouldn't move."

Naomi protested, "I made my decision. You can leave Esther in this miserable, dysfunctional house, but I'm staying with you or I'm moving out on my own. I'll be eighteen; you can't do anything about that."

"Naomi," Ruth warned. "There are things you don't understand, I—"

"I understand more than you think. I want to live with you," Naomi pleaded. "Please don't ask me to stay here."

Ruth knew she should say no, but between this and her cryptic text, she wasn't sure what Naomi knew and she needed to find out. Finally she nodded and said, "Until I go back to the city at least."

Esther looked at Ruth in panic and said, "I'm going with you too."

Ruth looked at Mum, who said nothing. She looked at Ruth in sheer defeat before rising and walking into the kitchen. Esther sat beside Ruth and took her hand in hers.

Ruth didn't trust herself to go after her mother. She would phone later, they would talk it out civilly, but Ruth couldn't risk a confrontation. She loved her mother, she truly did, and she didn't want to hurt her. It was only temporary, maybe even a few days. She would convince both the girls to go back home. Ruth wasn't sure how much time she had left, but she knew it was quickly running out.

Naomi didn't speak until they got to the house. Esther got out first, leaving the two of them to sit in the idling car. Ruth looked over at her sister, shutting the engine off. Naomi got out, adjusting her sling as she walked out into the snow. Ruth followed her, locking the car.

Naomi walked through the property, just to the edge of David's grove. She pointed with her good hand to the beginning of the tree line.

"I saw her about two weeks before he died," Naomi said. "I thought I was dreaming. She was naked, pale, and her feet barely touched the ground. It was like she was floating across the snow. I waited each night after that to try to see her. David was acting so strangely at the end. He was so jumpy...and always hungry. He would get up in the middle of the night a lot. I thought at first he was just in the kitchen...but four nights before he died, I saw him out there with her. Naked, pale like her. He was running, so fast, like he was at the Olympics. His hair started going white, like yours...and his teeth got sharper. Like yours."

Naomi turned to face her. "I knew it wasn't a bear when he died. I thought maybe I was just hallucinating, I thought it was all a dream. Then you rescued me."

"Why didn't you—"

"I didn't know if I could trust you," Naomi admitted. "David was...violent at the end. Anything could set him off and then he'd be screaming at us. He used to call me a lot of nasty names. Told me a few times I wasn't worth feeding and watering, like I was livestock. David never hit me—I don't think he hit Esther either—but you could tell he was thinking about it, like he was barely holding himself back. Like there was this tiny piece of him that was trying so hard to hold on, but too much of our brother was already gone. I was so afraid of David, but I'm not afraid of you."

Ruth shook her head. "You should be."

"Am I going to change, too?" Naomi asked.

"Did he bite you?"

She shook her head.

"Then I don't think so." Ruth held her sister to her and kissed the top of her head. "I will keep you safe," she promised. "You can stay here with me, but..."

"I'm not an idiot," Naomi replied. "If you go rabid, I'll shoot you."

Ruth chuckled, putting her arm around her. "That's my girl."

The hunger was strong that night, but she waited until the girls were in bed before she ransacked the house looking for food. She turned her phone on as she did so and it pinged at her three times in a row. She frowned and slid it open.

There were three messages from Ellie, and before even reading them Ruth guessed she had heard about the fire. Once she scrolled through them, her heart started skipping beats.

Ruth, call me.

Ruth, I'm scared, please call me.

Ruth, I really need to talk to you.

Ruth heard a whistling in the wind and instinctively she stood up, grabbing the rifle. Someone was there. Not Ellie. One of them.

She went outside, walking as softly as she could upon the snow. She saw a figure dart out of David's grove and she ran after it, chasing it over the fence. She had a glimpse of it and fired a warning shot into the air.

Ruth felt the presence slip away into the dark. She followed the trail for nearly an hour until she finally turned and headed back to the house. If this was some sort of trap to leave the girls vulnerable, she wasn't going to fall for it.

All the lights were on when she returned. She came in through the kitchen to see Esther sitting by the fire with—no, this had to be another hallucination.

"Ellie?" Ruth asked in shock. "What are you—"

"I need to talk to you," Ellie insisted. "Now."

Ruth agreed. "Okay. Esther, can you give us some space?"

Her youngest sister ran up the stairs, no doubt planning to sit at the top and eavesdrop. Ellie rose to her feet shakily and Ruth instinctively went to her side to steady her. Ellie placed her hand on Ruth's bicep, eyes widening at what she felt.

"You're a lot...bigger," Ellie commented, glancing between Ruth's arm and her eyes. "You're..."

"Jacked?" Ruth offered.

Ellie laughed nervously. "Yeah."

Ruth asked softly, "What's going on?"

Ellie swallowed hard. "I believe you. What you told me—I believe you now. And I... Rue, now it's my turn to tell you something unbelievable. I hope... God, this is going to sound crazy when I say it out loud and I really hope..."

Ruth took her hands in hers. "Ellie, whatever it is..."

Ellie confessed, "Rue, I'm pregnant."

CHAPTER TWELVE

Ellie had said it to her once before, over champagne flutes of ginger ale, in their little kitchen in Toronto. Ruth had felt the world quake beneath her feet in that moment, every priority suddenly shifting for a little bean barely sprouting. She loved an idea so much that it changed her entire life.

For a second, it was the same. The same joyous rush, then just as quickly, she was crippled by the realization of what that meant.

Ruth asked, "Are you sure?"

"I took three different tests. At first I thought I was just late but I felt so awful and I had a test lying around from last time so I... It was just so I would stop thinking about your story but then... Rue, if you're right, if you're becoming one of these things, then maybe being exposed to that venom through you... I haven't been with anyone else, not since the day we met. Maybe it's a tumor or an aneurysm, or maybe I'm losing it too."

Ruth started shaking and barely had the chance to sit down before she fell down.

"I'm so sorry," Ruth begged, "Ellie, if I had known, if I thought there was any chance. I bit you. I... God... God, this is all my fault. I should have told you all of it. I should have told you everything I knew, even if it was just lies that *thing* was telling me."

Ellie sat down beside her, tucking her knees up. "Then tell me now."

So Ruth did, repeating the events of the past weeks as best as she could remember. She left nothing out, not even her affair with Mishe. Ellie needed every piece of information she could get, pressing for details that Ruth wished she could offer. As it was, Ruth felt like she had said "I don't know" an ungodly number of times. She didn't know if anything Mishe had told her was factual. Mishe had said it was difficult for a Werros to get pregnant by a human but she hadn't said anything about the other way around. And even if she had, could Ruth have trusted that information? Mishe had been lying to her from the start. Why would the Werros tell the truth about this?

Ellie lost her cool after Ruth's third preface that it might all be a lie, telling Ruth to focus on what she did know.

And when Ruth ran out of facts, Ellie asked, "How do we find out for sure? Because if it's true, if I *am* pregnant because of some inexplicable monster magic..."

Ellie laced her fingers with hers and Ruth brought her into her lap. Ellie rested her head on her shoulder and Ruth kept her arms tightly around her.

Ruth murmured, "I meant what I said. I just want to be with you, baby or not."

Ellie confessed, "I know. And I know what I should do, if it's real, but I can't. I can't go through this again. I can't lose another one. I think it would break me."

Ruth closed her eyes, holding back tears. "Ellie..."

"I want this. I've never wanted anything as much as I've wanted to have a baby with you. I know... I know this is terrifying and I know I should be afraid, but I'm not."

Ruth lacked Ellie's strange calm; instead, horror filled her heart to the brim. This wasn't like Ellie. Ellie the skeptic, who didn't watch *Star Trek* because interstellar travel was too unrealistic for her. Why was she accepting this so easily? So willingly? Ruth hoped that maybe Ellie was humouring her, just until she could get Ruth to a hospital. But Ellie wouldn't have been so cruel as to bring a fake pregnancy into it. This had to be a blood bond, the venom twisting the love between them into parasitic manipulation. Ellie shouldn't still be here. She should have never been here at all.

Ruth had betrayed her and yet Ellie sat there with a worn smile and hope in her eyes.

Ruth murmured, "I love you, Ellie. I'm not going to let anything happen to you."

They stayed like that until Ellie fell asleep and Ruth carried her upstairs. She tucked her in before going back downstairs to douse the fire. She stood there at the hearth for a long time, trying to stop shaking. She wanted to take one of the expired Xanax in the bathroom, but she needed to be able to wake up if one of the Werros came back.

And then what? She was stronger now, but any time she had faced one it had wiped the floor with her. Now she had three people to protect and another on the way, one that might be human like Ellie or a monster like her. How had she allowed any of them to stay here with her? How had she done this to all of them?

Ruth took the rifle and sat by the door. She'd figure out what to do in the morning. Until then, she wasn't taking any chances with her family.

"Students are praising local woman Ruth MacGowan for her bravery during the fire, rescuing seven students and a teacher. MacGowan apparently ran into the fire by herself and is seen here carrying her own younger sister out. While the mayor has suggested that MacGowan might be publically decorated for her actions, the local firefighter chief would like to remind the public that fires are dangerous and should be left to the professionals. For Rogers, this is Heidi Chender."

Ruth shut off the TV, the still shot of her remaining for a second before the image faded. There was evidence now that she was alive. They would come soon with questions. That was alright. She had questions of her own.

Ruth slept through the day, waking just before dusk. Ellie had taken the girls out to lunch and had even sweetly brought back several raw cuts of meat. The poor pregnant vegetarian could be nowhere near Ruth while she ate them, but the gesture warmed Ruth's heart.

Near midnight, when both teens were in bed and Ellie was nodding off, Ruth took up the rifle again. Ellie stirred from the couch and looked up sleepily. Ruth bent down to give her a kiss and promised softly, "I'm just doing rounds. I'll be right back."

Ellie snuggled back into her blankets and Ruth took in the image of her by the fire. She smiled to herself before walking out the back door, locking it behind her.

For five days, she did the same, patrolling the forest line. After walking the perimeter several times, she would return to David's grove and remain there on guard until dawn broke. The nights were growing colder, the wind harsher, but the days were beginning to grow longer once more.

On the fifth night, Ruth was sitting against David's headstone, her eyelids growing heavy. The hunger had abated for a time, adjusting to its new cycle, but it was time for her to eat again. She would break her fast soon but the dawn was still far away and she had felt the creature's presence again. Not every night, but this night stronger than most. It was nearby. It wanted this place, David's grove, but it had yet to move.

It was closer now. Ruth could smell it. She rose to her feet and picked up her rifle. She aimed it toward the trees and waited. The wind died down as the creature stepped closer. The sky grew darker. Dawn would come soon, but not soon enough.

Ruth saw the Werros as it entered the grove. It was larger than Mishe and even fairer still. It cocked its head at Ruth and smiled widely, baring its teeth. Ruth recognized it. It was the one who had butchered a man in front of her. The one Ruth had tried to kill and failed.

"So it is as I thought. You live after all. Your scent has changed, human. I sense you stronger than before. Your blood sings differently. My sister will sense it as well, when she comes for you. And she will when she knows she failed to kill you."

Ruth touched the healed bite around her jaw. This creature's poison was in her too. It would be able to find Ruth if she ran.

It chuckled. "Yes, I would. Come on out then, Ruth MacGowan. If you are to try to kill me, put down that rifle and try to kill me as Werros. It seems hardly fair otherwise."

Ruth clicked the safety off. "For you or me?"

"If I wanted you dead, I would have done it when you first returned. Drop your gun, human. This does not have to end in violence."

Ruth smiled. "You're afraid of me."

"I am not afraid of your kind," it replied. "I killed the last of the Dorset in the Arctic and feasted on her heart with glee. Almost a thousand years, I have hunted humanity and thrived on your spilled blood. A girl in the forest alone is no threat to me."

"Then come at me," Ruth taunted, aiming the gun at it.

The creature moved fast, knocking Ruth onto her back before she could pull the trigger.

Ruth tried to reach for her gun but the creature bit into her arm. Ruth screamed out, pushing it off her, forcing it onto the ground with her weight. She bared her teeth, ripping into the skin of its neck. She gagged when she tasted blood, dark, heady, almost fermented. In her shock, she didn't notice the creature reach around, its teeth burrowing into her rib cage and piercing into the very marrow of her bones.

Ruth cried out, trying to kick the Werros from her, only gaining leverage when the impaled rib cracked in two. Ruth managed to push it off her, that second just long enough for her to roll onto her injured belly and start to crawl along the ice. The rogue creature grasped at her, wrapping its long fingers around her ankle. It began to drag her back, the loose rib further splintering, dangerously close to her lung. The thought was the only thing that kept Ruth from screaming in pain as she threw out her right arm, extending it long enough to capture the toe of the gun between her thumb and fore-finger.

The Werros drove its teeth through the back of Ruth's knee, its incisors under the shell of her patella. Ruth forced her hand to hold onto the stock of the gun, hyperextending her shoulder just to get all five fingers on the weapon. With the creature's next forceful bite, Ruth screamed out, grasping the polished wood as hard as she could, desperately trying to nudge the gun toward her. Venom pumped into her blood, her vision merging into a sickly haze just as she managed to grip the stock and yank the trigger guard into her numbing fingers.

With the last of her strength, she rolled all her weight onto her uninjured side, forcing the creature to raise itself high enough for Ruth to slap the barrel against its cheekbone and break its hold on her knee. It withdrew by a breath, coiling like a snake to strike again. Ruth dug the butt of the gun into the ice and thrust down, pro-pelling herself the vital inches away she needed to press the muzzle into the creature's belly and fire.

The Werros's eyes met hers, its pupils fading into pure white. It shuddered and tumbled onto the ground. Ruth fell onto her own back, gasping for breath. She looked over to see the Werros pulling itself to David's grave and resting its back against the headstone. Its blood dripped from its torso, almost solid, like little beads across the snow.

"You've won, human," it murmured. "I have waited too long to feed and you...you are stronger now. Sit, sit with me then. Do not be so cruel to let me die alone."

Ruth hesitated before rising shakily, barely making it a few steps before collapsing beside the creature. She flinched as the Werros stroked her face, its bone-white hand colder than ice.

"I see him in your eyes," it murmured. "You are so beautiful. I saw you through his memories, through his dreams. I see him alive again in you. I should have left long ago. They are hunting me, as they will hunt you. But I needed to return. I needed to see him once more."

"Did you kill my brother?" Ruth asked wearily.

The Werros whispered, "No. If you trust one thing, trust this. I loved him."

Ruth rested her head against the stone, closing her eyes as the Werros murmured, "I was hunting through the area when I first saw David. He was a broken man, but beautiful. I desired him, I lusted for his flesh and blood. I observed him for some time, watching from the forests. I had been alone for so long... I did not know how to pursue him, but then he found me first. He wasn't afraid. He thought I was a demon of some kind, some punishment for his past sins."

Ruth looked at the Werros, watching its blackest blood trail down its face as tears. The creature said, "We were happy, for a time. We had found peace together. But he had begun to change, becoming as you are now." It gave the ghost of a smile. "You would bear this burden alone if you could. You would walk away from everyone and everything you love to protect them from what you have become. But David was not as brave as you are and I was afraid to lose him. I sought the aid of my kin-circle. It was a mistake, a mistake that cost us both."

"What am I becoming?" Ruth demanded.

The Werros breathed out shakily. "A hybrid. The human genes are so much stronger than ours, but the poison corrupts, changes. You are closer to human than one of us, but...you will be stronger, faster. You will always thirst for blood, but it is never quenched as it as among our kind. The hybrids are more...virile. Among our females, we must drink a great deal of blood to conceive. But hybrids can sire a hybrid child with a human with a mere bite. If there were even a pair of you, it would take less than a human lifespan for you to outnumber us."

Ruth swallowed hard. "So they couldn't let him live."

It nodded, its shuddering growing worse. "Hybrids are killed immediately and without question. Any human showing any sign must be slayed. That is why your...your companion betrayed you. She was sent to find me. She killed David. She was meant to use you to find me, but instead corrupted you. She was supposed to kill you, but instead she created an even greater threat. Not only have you become a hybrid, but you have sired another one."

Ruth froze and it murmured, "I know. I can smell your mate on you. My sister will do the same. She will smell your spilled blood as I did and know...but if you slay her, you will be safe. We are the only two whose poison is in you. The others won't find you. Until then, any time you bleed, she will know where you are. You must stop her."

It shuddered, slipping from the stone. Ruth caught it and held it in her arms. It shivered, clinging onto Ruth's collar.

It murmured, "I wanted to die beside him. I wanted to lie down and die among his bones. But I couldn't break through the ice, not as weak as I was without his blood. It was all I wanted...all that I wanted..."

The creature said nothing more and Ruth realized it was dead. The Werros was light in her arms, as if whatever spirit it held weighed more than the being itself. She gently laid it atop David's grave and hobbled to the barnyard shed, returning with a shovel. She broke through the frozen ground, working as quick as she could as her body began the process of knitting her knee into something func-tional. The additional venom might have boosted her healing speed, but there was no telling if it was temporary or not. Ruth wasn't going to take the risk and slow down. She had to do this now herself.

The hole was shallow, but it was enough to protect the crea-ture from the elements. Ruth buried it without ceremony, tossing the frost-burnt soil on top of it like she was building a compost pile—didn't matter how things laid, it'd all be the dirt in the end.

When Ruth was done, she covered the disturbed earth with snow and very carefully rose back to her feet, her damaged knee shifting as it tried to pop back into place. She bowed her head, not knowing if the tears dripping down her face were from the pain or from grief, just knowing they'd freeze her eyelids shut if she kept at it. She wiped her face and stood, taking the gun as she limped across the field and back into her house, locking the door behind her.

Ellie stood in the kitchen, her housecoat wrapped around her, her hair tucked away in a matching cap. Ruth dropped everything and brought her into her arms. She kissed her desperately, clinging to her as close as she could, despite the shattered rib. The pain didn't matter, not as long as she could hold her.

Ruth heard the girls racing down the stairs and she took Ellie's hand, leading her back into the living room to meet them on the bottom steps.

"Was it out there?" Naomi demanded.

"A different one," Ruth said. "It's not going to be safe here for you. You need to leave. Ellie, take them to your brother's place in Ottawa. I'll meet you there when I can."

"What's going on?" Esther asked fearfully. "Why are you covered in blood?"

"Everything's fine," Ruth reassured them. "I'll just clean up—"

"No," Esther insisted. "You don't need to keep hiding things from me. We're in this together, whatever it is, like we've always been."

Ruth closed her eyes. "There are...things out there. Monsters. One of them killed David because he was...becoming like them. I've been poisoned, like he was. The one who hurt me knows I'm still alive. I need to find her and I... I'll do whatever I need to do to keep all of you safe."

Esther said nothing, thinking quietly to herself.

"Is the other one dead?" Naomi asked.

Ruth nodded. "I buried it in the back."

Esther asked finally, "Is this real?"

Ruth stood and took her hands in hers.

"I promise I will tell you everything, just not now," Ruth said. "Just trust me."

"We're not going anywhere," Naomi insisted. "That asshole took away my home once. I'll keep an eye out for us. I'll phone for help if I need to and I'm a better shot than you are. Just...just find that thing."

Ellie said gently, "It's almost daylight and you're shaking like a leaf. You need to eat and you need to get some sleep."

Ruth shook her head. "You need to get them out of here. They're going to be looking for both of us, El. If something happens to me, they're going to track you. I'm not going to let that happen. You all need to get out of here."

Ruth turned to Naomi, handing her the rifle. "You don't hesitate to shoot, no matter what. If you can take the shot, take the shot, even if I'm in it."

Naomi said nothing and tears streamed down her face.

Ruth sighed in relief. "Then you all need to get your things and go. I'll give you the biggest head start I can, but then you've got to keep going."

Ellie protested, "I won't leave you."

"We'll find each other again," Ruth promised. "I know we will."

She looked at her little family, the ones she loved most in the world. She was overwhelmed with the desire to protect them, to shelter them, to keep them safe. She had made a vow to all of them and she would die to keep it if she needed to. Ruth didn't need to make it out of this alive. She just needed to make sure Mishe didn't.

Ruth had killed twice now. She would do it again for them. For David. For herself. There would be no changing her mind, no hesitation. This ended tonight.

CHAPTER THIRTEEN

R UTH WALKED THROUGH THE snow unarmed. She stripped
herself of her gloves and hat, needing to be able to hear and
feel. She knelt down beside David's grave and the freshly buried
Werros and closed her eyes. She had been able to sense the other one
and Mishe and her had a bond.

Ruth thought of that night in the bar, the creature's teeth against
her skin, the violet eyes shining bright. She tried to relive it, tried to
feel it. Then she took out the bush knife she'd brought and sliced
down her hand, letting the blood drip down into the snow.

Ruth looked up at the sky and took a deep breath. The snow
began to fall around her as she stood. Ruth walked, her feet light on
the thickening snow.

The snow fell harder, blinding her. It went through her clothes,
dampening them. But the chill did not settle in her bones. She kept

walking. She felt the creature pulling toward her, felt the blood pumping in her body, and her jaw ached. The Werros was coming to her, but she would find her, slay her before she even stepped foot upon Ruth's land. It had taken one of her family. It would not take another.

Hours passed and it grew darker still. Ruth retreated back to the grove, worried that the monster must have slipped past her. As she walked back across the property, she felt a sudden rise in her blood pressure, her arms nearly burning. Her heart raced and her chest ached. She was here.

"So you do live."

Ruth turned, the Werros standing in front of her. The wind blew her translucent hair around her, shielding most of her slender frame. She cocked her head.

"You have changed," she said quietly. "It was as my kin-circle feared. You are not the human I left behind. I am not surprised. I felt your presence at times, but I thought it was just your blood haunting me. It was only when it returned to the earth that I could feel it. You are growing more and more like me."

Ruth growled, "I trusted you."

Mishe said, "That was your own choice to make. I came here for one purpose: to fix my sister's mistakes. Isala had made a monster that could destroy both of our peoples. She wouldn't end it, so I did for her. I thought the matter over, but Isala lost her mind in grief, devouring men like air. I returned to kill her, but she proved to be a wilder creature than I could manage on my own."

The Werros stepped forward, her eyes remaining fixed on Ruth's.

Mishe continued, "You have completed my mission for me, it seems. I smell the last of her life embedded in your skin. You held her while she died. I thank you for that act of compassion. I am sorry I couldn't give your brother the same end."

Ruth accused, "You tore him to shreds, Mishe. You gutted him."

"It was unpleasant, but necessary. It needed to look real."

"Same with seducing me, right?" Ruth asked angrily. "Unpleasant but necessary?"

"That was unplanned. I did not expect to be in your company for so long as to form an attachment. When I brought you to my kin-circle, I pleaded with Obe to bring you into our care, to let you live as an ally amongst us. To be a bridge between our world and yours, as there have been such before. When she told me what you were becoming, she ordered me to kill you. I did care for you, Ruth, but I have as much of a responsibility to my family as you do for yours. I have created you. It is my duty to destroy you. I do regret that you were brought into this but know that once you are dead, it will be over. My kin-circle need not know that I failed the first time."

Ruth suggested, "Unless I kill you."

The Werros rushed forward and threw Ruth to the ground, its hands around her throat. Ruth tried to cough, pushing against it. She managed to roll them over, pinning Mishe down beneath her. Mishe bit into her neck and Ruth cried out, trying to pull away. Ruth was tossed back into the snow, her hand instantly pressing against her throat, willing the bleeding to stop but knowing her luck was running out.

Mishe stood, its body softer, its eyes delicate again, its hips and breasts fuller. Ruth tried to slow her heart, but it jumped as Mishe grabbed her again, taking a long and agonizing drink from her bleeding throat before tossing Ruth back to the ground.

Mishe wiped its mouth. "Do not be hard on yourself, half-blood. If not me, another would find you. I can taste it in you now. You've already spread your disease, putting a parasite in the belly of the woman you claim to love. After I kill you, I will find her, and I will feast on their flesh."

Ruth threw herself at Mishe, slamming the creature into the snow. Ruth managed a hard blow into Mishe's jaw, knocking out a pair of teeth before the Werros grabbed her thigh. It raked its claws into Ruth, ripping through the clothes and flesh protecting Ruth's femoral artery. Ruth kicked into Mishe's distended belly, feeling the slosh of her own blood beneath the creature's skin. Mishe cried out and Ruth kicked again until her shredded leg was freed. She felt a second of relief before Mishe attacked her, its teeth ripping into Ruth's already flayed throat.

Ruth shuddered, the sensation in her hands and feet growing numb. Her body was slowing, easing into the draining, finding pleasure as she lost control of her senses. She felt pleasantly cool, as if a long fever had finally broken. Ruth arched her body toward Mishe, wanting to be closer to her, she who was her soulmate, her everything—

Adrenaline struck her like a hammer and suddenly Ruth surged forward, thrusting her arm hard against Mishe's chin, breaking the connection between them. Ruth rolled out from under it, halfway to kneeling before Mishe was upon her once more. Ruth fought the creature this time, thrashing and screaming. Ruth tore into it, ripping into the creature's flesh with her fingernails. Mishe sucked harder on Ruth's wound, as if coaxing the blood to spurt rapidly down the creature's own throat.

Ruth jerked her head, ripping her neck from Mishe's teeth, and managed to roll out from under it again. Without the venom, the puncture site bled freely, the flow of blood punctuated with each throb of her heart. Ruth's strength was nearly gone, but she forced herself to stand, pressing her hand hard against the wound.

Mishe let Ruth rise, as if allowing her a final dignity, before the Werros stood and bashed Ruth's body into the hard trunk of a cedar. The battery spiked down Ruth's spine, her fingers reaching back to grip into the rippled bark. She willed herself to stay upright, pleading with her broken body to let her die on her feet.

Ruth looked Mishe dead in the eye. She was gurgling too hard on her own blood to curse the creature, managing barely a "fuh" before she heard her rifle firing. She reflexively closed her eyes, opening them again to see Mishe crumple, Ruth's blood spilling from the dead Werros's lips as its corpse collapsed into the snow.

Ruth looked up, seeing a glimpse of Esther between the trees. Her young sister ran to her, tossing the rifle aside. Ruth tried to take a single step toward her but her butchered leg gave out, sending her crashing to the ground beside Mishe.

Esther knelt down, sitting Ruth up against her and burying her face in Ruth's hair. Ruth felt Esther's tears fall onto her bloodied face, could feel the vibrations of Esther's pleas against her fading pulse. Ruth wanted to turn her head, wanted to be able to see her baby sister's face one last time. But this was enough, more than enough.

Ruth murmured, "It's okay, baby. It's all right. It's all over now."

Esther sobbed and Ruth held onto her until she slipped into the dark.

CHAPTER FOURTEEN

RUTH WOKE IN NAOMI's bed, blinking as she once again took in the posters of a youth set ten years after her own. Every part of her body ached. Muscles that she didn't even know she had were crying out for the mere act of opening her eyes. A comforting voice said her name and Ruth stirred to consciousness, her heart easing in her chest at the sight of Ellie sitting on a chair beside her.

Ruth tried to speak, but Ellie interrupted gently, "Don't talk. You've got about twenty stitches and staples holding your throat together. It was hard enough to convince the ER nurses to let me take you home without getting bloodwork done. I'd rather not risk our luck a second time."

Ruth gave the slightest nod, but this too sent pain rippling down her chest. She could feel the rest of her sewn flesh now, each and every wire that had kept her together while she slept. None of these were designed to harmlessly melt into her skin as she healed. Ruth had been reinforced with rebar.

Ellie explained, "Esther said that she'd left her anxiety meds at Trip's place, so we went there first on our way out of town. But once we got there, Esther snuck out and stole his car. We made it here almost an hour after her. By the time we found you...Esther thought you were already dead. Trip and I got you into the car and drove straight to the hospital. You were under the knife less than ten minutes after we got there. You were out for sixteen hours. You woke for a little bit, though you probably don't remember that, but it was long enough to get you discharged. I think you met the on-call doctor before—Dr. Kaling?—she said that you'd be better off at home and didn't need to be monitored unless you wanted to be."

Ruth didn't like what the doctor's statement had implied but said nothing as Ellie concluded, "You've been in bed now for about a day, on and off. We had about half this conversation before. Do you remember?"

Ruth managed, "No."

Ellie took her bandaged hand in hers. "That's okay. Probably better if you don't. The main thing is, everyone's here and everyone's safe."

Ellie paused, looking toward the doorway where Esther was listening in. Ruth beamed at her, tears glistening in her eyes.

Ellie smiled softly. "I'm going to make everyone dinner. I'll be back in a bit with one of those disgusting meat slurries I keep finding in the freezer."

Ellie left the room and Esther rushed to the bed, jumping on and hugging Ruth tightly. Despite the pain, Ruth squeezed her back, nuzzling into Esther's hair as Esther buried her face into Ruth's uninjured shoulder.

Esther started crying and Ruth let her own tears flow. She held Esther at arm's length, looking in awe at her baby sister. Grown, strong, capable. The girl had stolen a car and driven it through a snowstorm, alone, and barely able to defend herself, ran out into the forests in order to save her sister from the elements and all the monsters they hid.

Ruth pressed her forehead to Esther's and whispered, "Thank you."

Esther sobbed harder, hiccupping like she had when she was a toddler and crying too hard for her little chest to handle. Ruth closed her eyes, breathing slowly, instinctively coaching Esther as she had when she was small.

Five seconds in, seven seconds out.

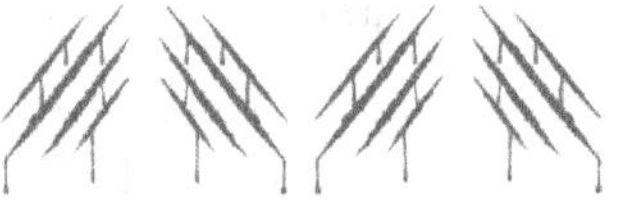

After another twenty-four hours, Ruth had healed enough to make it downstairs and have dinner with her family. Esther helped her into the kitchen, letting Ruth lean a little of her weight against her. Naomi already sat in a chair, the dog in her lap. She was talking with Ellie, who leaned against the counter, a cooling casserole at rest beside her.

Naomi cheered, "Look at that. My sister is a BAMF! One little measly vampire isn't going to knock her down. And Esther? Apparently an ace sniper. Us MacGowan girls, we don't take shit from no one."

Ruth rolled her eyes as she gingerly sat. "It wasn't a vampire."

"Whatever," Naomi said. "The main thing is that it's dead."

Ellie plated slices of the casserole and Esther helped her bring the meal over to the table. Ruth watched the domestic scene, her heart aching with what felt like ill-gotten contentment. She had won. Somehow, she had cheated death and received everything she had ever wanted. And yet...and yet...

Ruth exhaled sharply and all four looked to her.

"I'm fine," Ruth promised. "I just need to get some air. I'll be right back."

Ruth walked out the kitchen door on her own. The snow was still falling but now simply tumbling softly without the harsh winds to whip it across the landscape. She went through the yard, through the gardens and trees of her childhood, and came to where David rested.

Ruth knelt in front of his headstone, the creature's blood still frozen across his name. Ruth thought to scrape it off but left it. The Werros lay there too. Even Isala deserved some marker of having once lived and died.

Ruth whispered, "I don't know if I'm ever going to stop hating you, David. I'm not forgiving or forgetting anytime soon, but just... I loved you. I deserved better and in the end, you did too. So, if you're not too deep in hell to hear me...well, I'm sorry this happened to you. I'm sorry I got out and you didn't."

Ruth said nothing further, listening to the wind. They were alone now. Ruth and the monsters buried beneath her. Her hand went to her injured throat, wincing as she picked out another hanging piece of metal. Her body was healing so quickly that her staples had started popping out on their own.

It should have frightened her, thinking of her future as a hybrid, of being a wilder creature than both human and Werros combined. But in that moment, all she felt was bittersweet relief. It was over. For now, it was over.

ACKNOWLEDGEMENTS

Wilder Creatures would be nothing but the dyslexic ramblings of a madwoman without my incredible editor Rebecca Cuthbert. Your guidance and support have helped this novella shine in ways I never could have imagined. Thank you for your faith in me and bringing me along with you to Undertaker Books. Also, a massive thank you to your partners in crime, D.L. Winchester and Cyan LeBlanc, for taking such good care of my book.

Wilder Creatures was a long time in creation, but the last year of its development would not have been possible without the love and care I have received in my ongoing mental health recovery. As to not dox myself, I will keep these acknowledgments vague: thank you to my family doctor, my therapist, my out-patient care group, and to my sangha. A massive thank you to my family, both born to and those picked up along the way—with a special shout out to Audrey, beloved friend and human companion to the real-life Cora, who is indeed a very good girl.

And to end, my deepest gratitude to my dearest Christopher. I love you.

ADVANCE PRAISE FOR WILDER CREATURES

"A wild, bloody tale of love and betrayal that takes you by the throat and doesn't let go. Nadia Steven Rysing's Wilder Creatures is a hell of a ride."

-Elizabeth Broadbent, author of *Ink Vine* and *Ninety-Eight Sabers*

"Lots of *Wow, Wait, What?* moments in this intriguing story. The pace quickly ramps up and barrels full-speed, non-stop through plenty of action, mystery, and mystique. Will leave you wanting more."

-Ocean, author of the award-winning collection *I'm Not Scared...You Are*

"If you're tired of the same old vampires and were-wolves, never fear—Nadia Steven Rysing has created an original blood-sucking, same-sex reproducing, lesbian creature to haunt your nightmares. *Wilder Creatures* is a quick-paced novella with a few twists and turns I didn't see coming. With themes of strong family ties and a second-chance romance, there's something here for everyone. This one kept my attention to the end."

-Edale Lane, Amazon Best-selling author and winner of Rainbow, Lesfic Bard, and Imaginarium Awards.

About the Author

Nadia Steven Rysing (she/her) is a professional jack-of-all-trades living on the Haldimand Tract in Southwestern Ontario. Her work has appeared in a variety of anthologies, journals, and a zine floating around Albuquerque, New Mexico. You can find her reluctantly on X @a_tendency.